DANCING
IN THE
COSMOS

LOUISIANA STATE UNIVERSITY PRESS
BATON ROUGE

DANCING
IN
THE
COSMOS

FLOYD
SKLOOT

NEW & SELECTED POEMS, 1973–2024

Published by Louisiana State University Press
lsupress.org

Copyright © 2025 by Floyd Skloot

All rights reserved. Except in the case of brief quotations used in articles or reviews, no part of this publication may be reproduced or transmitted in any format or by any means without written permission of Louisiana State University Press.

LSU Press Paperback Original

DESIGNER: Michelle A. Neustrom
TYPEFACES: Whitman, text; Century Gothic, display

COVER ILLUSTRATION: *Sunlit Reflections,* 2008, by Beverly Hallberg.

LIBRARY OF CONGRESS CATALOGING-IN-PUBLICATION DATA

Names: Skloot, Floyd, author.
Title: Dancing in the cosmos : new and selected poems, 1973–2024 / Floyd Skloot.
Other titles: Dancing in the cosmos (Compilation)
Description: Baton Rouge : Louisiana State University Press, 2025.
Identifiers: LCCN 2025018302 (print) | LCCN 2025018303 (ebook) |
  ISBN 978-0-8071-8474-5 (paperback) | ISBN 978-0-8071-8528-5 (epub) |
  ISBN 978-0-8071-8529-2 (pdf)
Subjects: LCGFT: Poetry
Classification: LCC PS3569.K577 D36 2025 (print) | LCC PS3569.K577 (ebook) |
  DDC 811/.54—dc23/eng/20250611
LC record available at https://lccn.loc.gov/2025018302
LC ebook record available at https://lccn.loc.gov/2025018303

for Beverly

CONTENTS

ACKNOWLEDGMENTS xi

I. FROM *MUSIC APPRECIATION* (1994)

    Twilight Time 3
    Hazards 5
    My Daughter Considers Her Body 6
    You Asked for It 7

II. FROM *THE EVENING LIGHT* (2001)

    Argenteuil, 1874 11
    Seurat in Late Winter, 1891 13
    Oncogene 15
    Autumn Equinox 16
    Toomey's Diner 17
    Visiting Hour 18
    Slievemore 19
    Swans in Galway Bay 20
    Still Life with Eggs & Whisk 22
    Daybreak 23
    Flight 24

III. FROM *THE FIDDLER'S TRANCE* (2001)

    Wild Blackberries 27
    Celestial North 28
    The Yoga Exercise 29

Poppies 30
Behind Gershwin's Eyes 31
Starry Night 34
Frost 36
Dancing in the Cosmos 38

IV. FROM *APPROXIMATELY PARADISE* (2005)

The Role of a Lifetime 43
James McNeill Whistler at St. Ives, 1883 44
Under an August Moon 45
Lunch in the Alzheimer's Suite 46
Midnight in the Alzheimer's Suite 47
Salmon River Estuary 48
Amity Hills 49
The Juncos' Dance 51
Reese in Evening Shadow 52
Winter Solstice 54

V. FROM *THE END OF DREAMS* (2006)

A Hand of Casino, 1954 57
Poolside 59
Kansas, 1973 61
Breath 62
O'Connor at Andalusia, 1964 64
Whitman Pinch Hits, 1861 66
Latin Lessons 68
The End of Dreams 69
The Dance 70
The Hermit Thrush 71
Eliot in the Afternoon 72
Dowsing for Joy 76

VI. FROM *THE SNOW'S MUSIC* (2008)

Georges Braque in Pieces, May 1915 79
John Field in Russia, 1835 80

William Butler Yeats among the Ghosts 81
The Young Composers at Play, Westhampton, 1929 82
Balance 84
First Light, Late Winter 85
Transformations 86
Silent Music 87
Ezra Pound in a Spring Storm 88
Digging Zak's Grave 90

VII. FROM *CLOSE READING* (2014)

Jules Verne above Amiens, 1873 93
Paul Klee at Sixty 96
The Shared Room 97
Nostrand Avenue 98
My Grandparents' Dance 99
The Shore 100
Close Reading 101
Isaac Bashevis Singer in the Reading Room, 1968 104
In Thompson Woods with John Gardner, 1970 105
Sway 106
Painted Lady 108
At Rowan Oak 109

VIII. FROM *APPROACHING WINTER* (2015)

My Grandfather's Final Day in the Old Country, 1892 113
October 30, 1938 114
Dream of a Childhood 116
Handspun 118
Approaching Winter 119
Crying over "Scarlet Ribbons" 121
Today 122
Dylan Thomas at Sundown, November 9, 1953 123
Samuel Beckett Throws Out the First Pitch 124
Sightings 126
Lost in the Memory Palace 127
Thomas Hardy in the Dorset County Museum 129

IX. FROM *FAR WEST* (2019)

    The Lost Name 133
    Tangled 134
    Over and Over 135
    Jet Song 137
    Chris Cagle Is Dead 138
    At Last 144
    Nabokov in Goal, Cambridge, 1919 145
    Jules Verne at Safeco Field, Seattle, Spring 2014 146
    Childe Hassam at the Oregon Coast, Summer 1904 148
    Yahrzeit 150
    Island 154
    Life Bird 155
    Sky Dance 157

X. NEW POEMS (2016–2024)

    Parkinson's 161
    Early Winter by the Fire 168
    Pine Ridge 169
    Freestone Peaches 170
    Apartment 4M 172
    Brooklyn, 1957 173
    After Terminating Dialysis, June 1997 174
    Living Night 175

NOTES 177

ACKNOWLEDGMENTS

These poems were selected from the following volumes:

Music Appreciation (1994); *The Evening Light* (2001); *The Fiddler's Trance* (2001); *Approximately Paradise* (2005); *The End of Dreams* (2006); *The Snow's Music* (2008); *Close Reading* (2014); *Approaching Winter* (2015); and *Far West* (2019).

Some sections of "Parkinson's" were previously published in different forms in the following journals: *American Journal of Poetry, Boulevard, Hopkins Review,* and *Plume.*

Some of the new poems were previously published in the following journals: *Boulevard:* "After Terminating Dialysis, June 1997"; *The Galway Review* (Ireland): "Living Night"; *On the Seawall:* "Early Winter by the Fire"; *Hopkins Review:* "Freestone Peaches"; *Southern Review:* "Apartment 4M"; *Plume Poetry:* "Brooklyn, 1957"; *Tiferet:* "Living Night."

I.

FROM *MUSIC APPRECIATION*
(1994)

Twilight Time

The Platters
Spring, 1958

It could only be
a dream since the drapes
are tied back, there is lilac
sunset above rooftops and Sabbath
candles flicker in their saucers
just for play. How else
could there be rhythm
and blues on the Victrola
at dusk? My mother softly
sets the needle arm down
and turns to smile at him
through the static, spreading
her feathered boa like angels'
wings before gliding
into my father's arms.

His easy chair has floated
away, the sea of carpet
has parted and oak dark
as the earth's heart holds
them. I know it is only
in dreams that their hands
touch and twine, that shades
of night would bring them
together like this.
All that is impossible
is that it could have happened.

They move to the smooth blend
of the singers' voices, love
is in their eyes, their separate

days are given up to a mellow
music. Now they are twirling,
together at last at twilight time.

Hazards

Stiffly, without flutter,
her dresses, jeans,
and creepers move
in the fall breeze.
She toddles beside me
pointing to jays on
the roof until the walk
ends, spilling her face
first in the grass.

I have seen cars
spinning toward her,
buses sucking her under
as she reaches up for me.
Derailed trains flip,
bounce twice, coming.
From left field, I have
seen fouls crack her soft
skull, seen dogs attack, bats
fly end over end to find
the blanket where she sits.

She is up, clutching
my finger, steadied.
A squirrel bursts from fence
to tree. She lets go
and moves toward it,
laughing, waving.

My Daughter Considers Her Body

She examines her hand, fingers spread wide.
Seated, she bends over her crossed legs
to search for specks or scars and cannot hide
her awe when any mark is found. She begs
me to look, twisting before her mirror,
at some tiny bruise on her hucklebone.
Barely awake, she studies creases her
arm developed as she slept. She has grown
entranced with blemish, begun to know
her body's facility for being
flawed. She does not trust its will to grow
whole again, but may learn that too, freeing
herself to accept the body's deep thirst
for risk. Learning to touch her wounds comes first.

You Asked for It

Show me film clips of William McKinley.
Show me Charles Atlas pulling six autos
down two miles of road. I would like to see
the vault at Fort Knox, chimps with hammertoes,
a man boning chickens while blindfolded.

Show me Ebeye Atoll, near Kwajalein,
worst slum in the Pacific. Show me red
squill being made into rat poison, pain-
free surgery as performed in Shansi,
old friends playing poker underwater.

Then show me love as it was meant to be.
Show me an old man and his grown daughter
walking alone near a cranberry bog,
not the Robot Man and his Robot Dog.

II.

FROM *THE EVENING LIGHT*

(2001)

Argenteuil, 1874

As summer sun stipples the garden grass,
Monet is watering his roses. Camille sits
in the noon light, chin on hand, white dress
a pillow for young Jean who no longer fits
across her lap. Missing the city, she
is ready to pack right now if only Claude
could tear himself away. But she knows he
wants to spend time painting with Edouard,
and Jean, half asleep, is already talking about
having a picnic tomorrow. It is always
like this. Now Claude has brought his paints out
to sit beside Edouard and work till day's
end. At least he is turned away from her.

She sees what will happen even before
Pierre arrives. There is no wind to stir
the air, no cloud to change the light; what more
could they hope for? These are men who would paint
their wives on deathbeds if the light were right.
Camille smiles and shifts Jean so that his weight
Is off her thigh. Oh, they will eat fish tonight,
a red mullet or, better still, fresh eel,
only in her dreams. Perhaps they should
eat this hen and cock clucking at their heels.

After the last Salon, of course the men would
need something like this, a slow summer to
paint their hearts out, a blossoming of sheer
joy together. So there is nothing to do
but hold still in the heat and be here
with all one's heart—perhaps a quick flutter
of the fan to keep Jean calm and herself
fresh—as time slows and the men in utter
concentration, begin to lose themselves

in the closed circle of their art and Manet
paints the Monets in their garden as Monet
paints a grinning Manet painting the Monets
in their garden and Renoir paints the Monets
in their garden in the summer in Argenteuil.

Seurat in Late Winter, 1891

*Georges Seurat died of diphtheria in Paris, March 29, 1891.
He was 31.*

In the Pointillist painting of Georges Seurat
the precise placement of dots of pure color
forces a viewer's eyes to mix them much as
paint on a palette, thereby demonstrating

art's truly mutual nature. Surrounded
by paint pots, Seurat stands too close to his huge
canvas to see the effect he seeks, but that
does not matter. In fact, it is the essence

of what he has been trying to show! He holds
a half dozen brushes between his knuckles
or gripped in his teeth, head teeming with theory.
The way light truly is, the way distance works

on a wave, the way the mind lies to the eyes—
if he can only get it right, there will be
a science of art, perception exactly
reenacted in all its perfect pleasure.

But Seurat is not well. He would like to tell
Signac how close he is to the exquisite
balance at last. He would like to see the look
on Pissarro's face as he is overcome

by amazement. He would like for his mother
to know his child now; she should meet the woman
he has loved and hidden away. He would like
to rest, swallow without pain, breathe with the old

ease. He spreads his fingers to let the brushes
clatter to their rack, plucks one from his mouth, steps
forward. Yellow ocher for the earth. Next comes
a field of green. He thought there would be more time.

Oncogene

Before eyes, before eye color, before
fingers, before breath and cry, it was there.
Nothing to be seen or touched, something more
like a current, a stirring of the air.

When he stood by his desk in second grade
muttering through the pledge of allegiance,
it was there. At ten, the first time he played
cello solos before an audience,

it was there. A readiness in the cells,
an occult passion for growth. When he dreamed,
it was there as the secrets a ghost tells
while the wind shifts. In moonlight as it gleamed

through lids half open in his sleep, it was there.
It was there when he ran beside a creek
at first light, taking the sharp winter air
into the soft tissue of lungs grown weak

now, though he is only forty years old,
though he was strong, though it began somewhere
deep in his bones. That day when he was told,
he already knew. It was always there.

Autumn Equinox

I feel my body letting go of light
drawn to the wisdom of a harvest moon.
I feel it welcome the lengthening night
like a lover in early afternoon.

My dreams are windfall in a field gone wild.
I gather them through the lengthening night
and when they have all been carefully piled
my body begins letting go of light.

Indian summer to leaf-fall to first frost
the memories that were carefully piled
become the dreams most likely to be lost.
My dreams are windfall in a field gone wild

now that memory has abandoned them,
now that Indian summer, leaf-fall, first frost
have become the same amazing autumn
skein of those dreams most likely to be lost.

I feel my body letting go of light.
I feel it welcome the lengthening night,
the windfall of dreams that have long been lost
to Indian summer, leaf-fall, and first frost.

Toomey's Diner

Sundays at dawn were whispers and silent
pissing on the inside of the privy bowl.
If belt buckles merely clicked, zippers
crept shut, and the heels of heavy shoes
only thudded together muffled in our hands,
mother slept on as we slipped out the door.

Sunday mornings my face seemed to melt
in ripples of chrome circling high stools
at the bar of Toomey's Diner. The air
inside was thick with breath and smokes
as I spun between my father and brother
waiting for our *flapjacks all around*.
I saw the soles of my feet turned upside
down in the stools' silvery pedestals
and knew enough to spin without a squeak.

So this was the world outside. Red leather
to sit on, red Formica edged in chrome
where my elbows fit, red menus studded
with paper clips. Signs said Special Today.
This was the stuff of weekday dreams. A small
jukebox at every table, rice to keep
the salt dry, toothpicks, a great pyramid
of cereal boxes hiding the cook.
Sunday was sizzling grease and apple juice
glowing pink, then blue in the sudden shift
of neon. Sunday laughter gave off such
heat that walls burst with sweat.

When the day came apart, I always had
the relative silence of knives and forks
on plates, the delicate lids of syrup holders
snapping shut, coffee slurped from steaming mugs,
coins on the counter, the sound of our bill
skewered by Toomey as we turned to leave.

Visiting Hour

We came straight from school,
crossing the island as winds
rose and fell. From half
a mile away the whitecapped
baywater smelled of fuel oil,
marsh grass, and autumn
darkness. Gulls circled
a trawler nudging the dock.
We gathered in an alley
behind the old hospital
where our fathers recovered,
or declined, or lingered
behind the cold panes keeping
them from us. We were too young
and full of dangerous life
to be allowed inside. Stroke,
cancer of the lung, a broken
hip, severed arm, failing heart.
We named our fathers by what held
them there. Clot, stone, spine.
Taking turns to stand on one
another's shoulders, we tapped
on windows as the sun set.
Fathers smiled within the folds
of their faces, waved, lay back
among the pillows. They turned
white before our eyes, became
quiet behind glass in their
gleaming ground-floor rooms.

Slievemore

Achill Island, Ireland

This is where the sea of my childhood ends,
a cone of quartz and mica where sheep graze
above the golden curve of Dugort Strand
and tombs that date to the New Stone Age.

This is what I was looking towards those nights
I left the shouting behind to stand where
surf drew back into itself and streetlights
from home grew dimmer in the salty air.

In the galaxy of the wave I could
travel to the ocean's outer reaches
with one deep breath. In a raft of driftwood
I could land on the deserted beaches

of villages cloaked in mist. They all looked
like this. Small white houses to welcome me
under weathered crags like Slievemore, fleece hooked
on gorse, moorgrass swaying, and a calm sea.

Swans in Galway Bay

Seven pairs of swans preen
this morning near the docks.
We walk down together
searching among the rocks
for a perfect feather
to commemorate the scene.

The swans float, one foot still
tucked underneath a wing,
the other held steady
as a rudder. They seem
both unconcerned and ready
for whatever the day will

bring them as they drift past.
Soon they are swept away
in pairs where the River
Corrib surges into Galway Bay—
from here just a sliver
of jagged slate-blue glass

but fierce enough to spin
them sideways toward the sea.
Paired still, they carry on
their slow ceremonies,
adjusting with utter calm
to the currents they move in,

content, it would appear,
to end up wherever
they find themselves as long
as they are together,
each feather where it belongs,
each mate with a clear

line of sight to the other.
We have come to the docks'
end empty-handed. I turn
back, but she stops to watch,
holding me there as one
small feather drifts to shore.

Still Life with Eggs & Whisk

Eggs on a white background, eggs in a glass
bowl, and a whisk twined in its own shadow.
She works with shade and light getting the mass
and depth right, bringing the late morning glow
that warms our house on clear November days
down to drench the delicate surfaces
of these half dozen eggs that hold her gaze.

They turn the yellow of ground irises
where warmth within them rises to the shell
and now it is time for the air around
them to seep lavender. Soon I can smell
it, the pungent herb of love, and the sound
filling the room as she paints is the same
sound hearts might make when they burst into flame.

Daybreak

The shapes that moved outside
our door tonight were four deer
come to feed on the last winter
weeds. The riot of their flight
seemed to echo through the dark
when I left my bed to see them.

Now the valley sends it voices
up through morning mist. Cows low,
the sheep farmer's old border
collie barks as she herds strays,
and the southbound freight is
an hour late. Where our hillside
plummets, a fringe of feathery
wild grasses webbed with frost
bends as though lost in prayer.

My wife built this house round
because a clear loop of moonlight
found the space for her early
on a morning like this. She woke
in her down sleeping bag under
a canopy of second growth to hear
great horned owls call from oaks
creaking in a sudden surge of wind.
When she sat up, there was a deer
standing exactly where a dowser
had told her the well should go.

Flight

The summer night is flying
by, rattling windows where light
is alive. Bats are shadows,
brilliant flickers in a mist
of insects, and bumblebees
circle the hyssop. The air
thickens. Directly above
us now a small plane crosses
the horizon of the half
moon on its way to the sea.

This is a night even deer
might soar. We believe they are
searching for a wind somewhere
within the thicket of wild
rose, hazel, and blackberries.
We believe the dark whisper
of grasses to be an owl's
wing pulse, the drift of oak leaves
an echo of shifting tides
from beyond the Coast Range.

As silence glides in gentle
spirals back to the earth, first
the sheen, then the shock of all
we have seen comes clear. This is
the moment we know pure flight
has little to do with lift
or drag and much to do with
dreams. It is the moment we
turn together to begin
our own powerful ascent.

III.

FROM *THE FIDDLER'S TRANCE*

(2001)

Wild Blackberries

in memory of my brother

In mid-July the blackberries were tart
and firm within their sweet surrounding flesh.
The full day's sun had just begun to mark
itself on the hidden red as a wish
for time, one week more at most, and warm nights
without rain. Thorns, leaves simple and lobed, dew
poised on dark branch tips framing the last white
flowers: everything reminded me of you
at the end, in a thicket of tubes, blood
spun clean for one more day, glistening hair
suddenly gray in a fan around your head.

The solstice brought a drenching rain as light
left summer behind. Berries draped with mold
shriveled to their stems and vines seemed to fold
in on themselves like dreams under the weight
of swarming yellowjackets. Here and there,
especially if my eyes were closed, I caught
a whiff of missing sweetness in the air.

Celestial North

Nights like this you could tell me time
is porous as gauze and I would believe
you. Tell me tonight has always happened
and always will be happening, since nothing
I know any longer says No. Whisper it
and I would believe you. Tonight the breeze
cooling us comes from the place where dreams
are harbored. Say this moment when winter
swivels into spring is genesis writ small,
say light is the center of darkness,
and I would turn toward it like a flower,
following your hand across the heavens
as it finds the north celestial pole.

The Yoga Exercise

Within a rushing stream of morning light
she stands still as a heron with one sole
held flush against the other inner thigh
and her long arms like bony wings folded
back so that when the motion of a breeze
passes through her body there is a deep

repose at its root and in an eye's blink
she has become this gently swaying tree
stirring in the wind of its breath while linked
to ground by the slow flow of energy
that brings her limbs together now in prayer
and blessing for the peace she is finding there.

Poppies

For years after a blaze, tree poppies
will spread brilliant yellow flowers
like the echo of flames in chaparral.
Camouflaged among crumbling bones of earth,
the pale salmon petals of pygmy poppies
thrive in thin alpine air. I have seen
acres of Oregon rainbows given over
to blind buds in hot southern sunlight,
cream cups tip their teeming bowls under
a sundown wind, and prickly poppies turn
back cattle grazing a north Texas pasture.
I have been where winter rains stitch
a patchwork of Amapola del Campo
on the spring countryside. So I love
the moment your eyes close, when you become
the fire poppy whose buds must droop
before its flushed flowers will open.

Behind Gershwin's Eyes

They did not believe him.
They told him the smell
of burning garbage was all
in his head. Some mornings
it was all he could do
to lift his head from
the pillow. Some nights
his brain was on fire,
songs he thought would take
a hundred years to write
suddenly aflame behind
his bulging eyes.

Dizzy in the barber's
chair, dizzy before
the chorus, dizzy
on the tennis court.

They did not believe him
even when he was adrift
in the first movement
of his Concerto in F.
He felt darkness beyond
the footlights seep
into his soul, nothing
but a sea of dream
everywhere, and heard
the echo of unplucked
strings, a quiver
of timpani dying out
quickly as one long
note from an oboe
wafted heavenward.
Then he found himself
back in Los Angeles,

familiar body still
upright on the piano stool,
Smallens with his baton
frozen at the shoulder,
only to blunder again
in the andante, and they
told him nothing was wrong.

Dizzy in the Brown
Derby, dizzy before
the surf, dizzy
in the swimming pool.

They believed he was
not happy in Hollywood.
*There is nothing wrong
with Gershwin that a song
hit wouldn't cure.*
It was in his head, he was
lovelorn or he was riddled
with guilt, he was balding
and drooling, muddle-headed
by noon, listless underneath
the stars. They believed
him sapped by motion-picture
making, and longing for New
York City. Those hands
once a blur on the keyboard
could only move slow as flowers
toward the sun yet nothing
was wrong. In the spring
those sandaled feet
that could only shuffle
in the summer garden

had been quick as flame
to his own new music
yet nothing was wrong.

A blade of light
where the drawn shades
meet. Roses without odor,
ice water leaping from its cut
glass goblet, eyes leached
of luster in the shadowy
mirror of his brother's eyes.
He spread chocolates melted
in the oven of his palm
up his arms like an ointment,
and soon he was gone.

Starry Night

> Perhaps I might really recover if I were in the country for a time.
> —Vincent van Gogh

Tonight the moon throbs with light
it seizes from stars as they rise
and the cypresses grow holy
before my eyes. Wind fills the sky.
I see clouds shudder, houses
and shops cower, but somehow
high grass finds its own source
of stillness. I think it is violet
in nature. Never has there
been such a night for seeing
how the dark world thrives
when day's brilliance dies
and sight fully becomes surprise.

Who would want all these deep blues
to soften as though toward dawn?
No dawn will bring along
a day as pure again. Who would
want to be well enough to lose
such hues? I know a man can
be so far from madness the true
world cannot find him. I know
he will be saved only when
the moon collects enough radiance
to render heaven tangible
as the breath of sunflowers.

Look: there is a glow inside
the emptiest spaces when we
study their darknesses. There is
also a hush no stroke of
a painter's brush can muffle.

Think of the instant swallows
rising above a field you enter
suddenly loop back in unison—
a thick landscape of faith
that is beyond words, yet explains
why I am standing here at all.

Frost

Wizened, spoiling for a fight, Frost is here
again. I have tried adjusting my pain
medication and sleep schedule, but still
he comes back to wander these woods like wind
stirring the Douglas fir. There is a gleam
of cold light where he stops and squats to track
the cries of naked oak that lean against
a surge of squalls.
                I hear him rhyming oak
with choke, then smoke and cloak as he looks down
into the valley. It will grow slowly
visible with the lifting of morning
mist and he will allow himself a small
smile. Spoke. Broke.
                Finally he turns to me,
lifting his chin to indicate the rough
grove at my back. "I see you lost your bees."
I nod as though I always speak with ghosts.
"They were gone before I got here."
                          Frost first
showed up with late September's heavy rain,
a creature of the equinox, I thought,
till I got a closer look. He follows
his own timetable like the pack of deer
that comes and goes now hunting season has
ended.
        "You need some chickens," he whispers.
"Good layers kept me and mine alive through
lean years." He leads me straight uphill. Baroque.
Folk. Roanoke. "Awoke," I say and he
stops dead to let me know who makes the rules.

Then his face unfolds, thawing as he seems
to grow young before my eyes. "Like your cane,"
he says, and winks when he adds "don't tell me:

Hazel from Rapallo in honor of
Ezra Pound." He shakes his shaggy head. Yoke.
Hoax. "They let him go when I told them to."

Because I have been reading Freud I know
this is the key. First illness, then prison,
then being freed by Frost. Wish fulfillment,
the heart of every dream. He makes his way
toward a pile of pine and points to the axe.
Stroke. Soak. "Running low." I turn to find him
drifting west with the sun and well beyond
reach of my voice. "There is more seasoning
behind the gazebo," I tell thin air
and watch another morning shape itself
around the twist of winter on the wind.

Dancing in the Cosmos

At first I thought the new
moon was pulling us straight
toward the cosmos in bloom
and singing at your yard's
edge. Then I heard the tune
rising. We began to swirl
in a warm whirlwind, sheer
scarves encircling us
like the visible scent
of snapdragons and sword
lilies all crimson, pink,
and yellow where your hillside
buckles valleyward.

A sudden shift in tempo
let us spare the lacy
crowns of fennel bent
to our waists by the weight
of their seeds and left us
meshed in raspberry vines.
One look and again I knew
we would soon be hopelessly
deep in the feathers
and petals of the cosmos.

But I believed the music
filling the night was saying Give
in, spin through the cosmos
with faith we will not harm
even the palest wildflower
with our inspired capers.
I believed because the clear
sky we slept under this summer
was still teeming with wild
harmonies. Bats swooped

to owl shrieks and the Milky
Way soaked up the moon's
last offering of light.
So the land was going dry.
So the sun was hotter than ever.
Such nights, such alien dancing,
and never did we lose
a single frilled floret.

IV.

FROM *APPROXIMATELY PARADISE*

(2005)

The Role of a Lifetime

> I am bound upon a wheel of fire . . .
> —King Lear

He could not imagine himself as Lear.
He could do age. He could rage on a heath.
Wounded pride, a man gone wild: he could be clear
on those, stalking the stage, ranting beneath
a moon tinged red. Let words rather than full-
throated roars carry fury while the wind
howled. He could do that. And the awful pull
of the lost daughter, the old man more sinned
against than sinning. The whole wheel of fire
thing. But not play a wayward mind! Be cut
to the brains, strange to himself, his entire
soul wrenched free, then remember his lines but
act forgetting. Understand pure nonsense
well enough to make no sense when saying
it. Wits turned was one thing; wits in absence
performed with wit was something else. Playing
Lear would force him to inhabit his fear,
fathom the future he had almost reached
already. Why, just last week, running here
and there to find lost keys, a friend's name leached
from memory. Gone. No, nor could he bring
himself to speak the plain and awful line
that shows the man within the shattered king:
I fear I am not in my perfect mind.

James McNeill Whistler at St. Ives, 1883

Whistler needs no one to sit for him now.
He is finished with portraits, with people.
Finished with nocturnes too, soft edges,
the muted light of a coastal fogscape.
He needs surprise. He wants to be outside
with a panel of wood, a thumb box of colors
and brushes, and nothing to hold him in place.
Bring on the war of sea and shore, clouds
blown apart. Autumn daylight like a shock
to the heart stirs him to life. He is after
the spontaneity of a breaker turned back
on itself. What is a whitecap but a stroke
of wind on wave, the Lord's own breath
in a flash of foam? Away too long from storm,
from the sea's surge, he feels himself awaken
before the horizon's shifting form, where time
itself is visible to the naked eye, where a ship
caught in a trough struggles to right itself.

Under an August Moon

This is the Green Corn Moon. This is the end
of summer rising with heat in its fat red fist.
Stars shoot through the night. The trend is
toward lingering high pressure off the coast.
By day, flat blue skies; by night, stillness
growing darker, denser. Power fails.
Mars has come near and looms to the south.
There is something starker than ever
to this August, an eloquence in its fever pitch.
Speech fails to convince. We want thunder
and heavy rain but get lightning strikes
and wildfires. The peace is broken,
deserts of the east in flames, the west
torrid with terror. Promise turns threat
and the heavens press upon us.
This is the error of our ways.
The corn crop stands scorched in its ears.
The sun saying we have learned nothing
will stare us down in the morning.

Lunch in the Alzheimer's Suite

My mother smiles at me. She reaches out
to touch my face and wonders who I am.
The fleck of tuna dangling from her mouth
falls as she asks, "Can you find me a man?"
Swaying willow and afternoon drizzle
fracture the light that falls across her tray.
Her hands, as though assembling the puzzle
lunch has become, adjust fork, bowl, and plate,
adrift in shadows. Sometimes she forgets
to swallow. Sometimes she holds a spoonful
of soup in the air and loses herself
in its spiraling steam. In a whirlpool
of confusion she may suddenly sink
in her seat and chew nothing but thin air.
She is fading away. Her eyes grow dark
as she looks at the old man sitting there
claiming to be her son. She slowly shakes
her head, lifts an empty cup and drinks.

Midnight in the Alzheimer's Suite

Lost in the midnight stillness, my mother
rises to dress and begin another
chilly day. She crosses the moonlit floor.
There is too much silence beyond the door,
and a lack of good cheer, so she breaks
into song. But the coiling lyric snakes
back on itself and tangles in her throat.
She stops long enough to see a cloud float
along the hall, but somehow the cloud speaks
in the voice of the night nurse. Someone peeks
from a doorway. Now someone starts to moan,
someone else coughs and my mother's stray song
returns for a moment: *oh you belong
to me!* If the audience would quiet
down, she would remember. Opening night,
that's what this must be, and the curtain parts,
and the spotlight is on, the music starts,
but there is too much movement, too much noise,
yet she cannot stop, must maintain her poise,
smile and keep on singing. Then it must be
over because the night nurse is there, she
embraces my mother and leads her back
offstage, whispering, bringing down the dark
again. Tired, but pleased with her last set,
my mother lies down for a well-earned rest.

Salmon River Estuary

Drifting close to shore, we enter the shadow
of Cascade Head. Our kayak jitters in an eddy
as we dip and lift the double-bladed paddles
to keep ourselves steady. Lit by morning sun,
current and rising tide collide before our eyes
in swirls of foam where the river becomes
the sea. Surf seethes across a crescent of sand.
Gone now the bald eagle's scream as it leaves
a treetop aerie, the kingfisher's woody rattle,
gulls' cackle, wind's hiss through mossy brush.
Light flashing through sea mist forges a shaft
of color that arcs a moment toward the horizon
and is gone. Without speaking, moving together,
we power ourselves out of the calmer dark
and stroke hard for the water's bright center
where the spring tide will carry us back upriver.

Amity Hills

I came here uneasy with the strange ways of forest life,
the crying sound of a white oak swaying in winter wind,
      mellow huff of deer settling to sleep
          on a slope, the soft rain—
      after sunset has spread like a stain—
becoming sudden storm rushing through the valley as night
falls, or the steady return of wildness across a thin
      margin we have made to keep
ourselves still within the seasons' wax and wane.

And I was slow to fathom the loudmouth tree frogs' bright green
exuberance in underbrush as the pond rose with March
      runoff. Never knew what fog looked like
          from above, or how it seeped
      through leaves like the spirit of a breeze.
What dawnlight does to the dew trapped on a torn windowscreen.
I had not slept outdoors or lost myself under an arch
      of fir and climbed the hillside's
      contours home. I never felt as free

as the evening grosbeak bursting like flame from a snowdrift
in late November, as the maple trapped in its cycle
      of reddening but soon enough to
          begin budding. Life was slow
      to change here but change would go
on endlessly, and seldom seemed to change pace. Morning mist
sometimes formed itself into a blazing rainbowed circle
      above our house and would do
      a kind of dance before it was through

with us. I never knew how connected weather was to
the tint of leaf, or light was to where coyote crossed a hill,
      time was to the space a forest claimed
          for deadfall. Till, near fifty,
      I finally left the city

and went to be with my love in her round house in the woods,
where soil was hard, water deep, and the late June air was cool.
                We live where nothing is tame,
     above a small town called Amity

at the stony end of an ancient lava flow, on massed
rock left by Ice Age floods. Poison oak and blackberry vines
        thrive here. By year's end a creek will rise
              from the hill's heart and pour
     for six months upon the valley floor,
dwindling back underground when the summer solstice has passed.
Time here has drawn me out beyond strangeness. Or drawn me in.
              I have learned that surprise
    is not always shock and nothing to fear,

that the dark-eyed juncos throng when wild fennel goes to seed,
that Indian summer can color the landscape of dreams
       gold through a winter of freeze and thaw,
           that the pattern of wind
    and the way old growth trees have been thinned
together help a harsh September rain carve itself deep
into the ridge exactly where evening sun always seems
             to soften the least flaw
    in all we see before the dark begins.

The Juncos' Dance

Trilling in the early April light,
a flock of dark-eyed juncos flits
from swaying feeder to lilac
to sword fern to cedar sapling
and back. A solitary jay watches
from his barberry perch, bobbing
as though in time to their reel.
I have seen him commandeer
the feeder, scattering sunflower
seeds and millet in moody squalls,
twitching his crest in triumph,
one grain caught in his beak.
I have heard his call, this brash
punk, a voice half hawk, half crow.
But now, his blue-gray feathers lit
by morning sun, he simply sits,
mesmerized before the common
elegance of the juncos' dance.

Reese in Evening Shadow

I prayed for easy grounders
when Pee Wee Reese fielded,
hanging curves when he hit.
At Ebbets Field, in late August
of my eighth year, I watched
him drift under a windblown
pop fly, moving from sunlight
to shadow as he drew near home.

Now, on the first anniversary
of his death, the August night
is wild with mosquitos and bats,
skunk in the compost. A pack of deer
thrashes through tangled hazel
and poison oak as they cross the hill
below its crest in search of water.

Nursing the day's final herbal
concoction against joint pain
and lost sleep, the same drink
I have used all twelve years
of my illness, I tilt my head back
in its battered Dodgers cap to rest
against the slats of an Adirondack chair

as a screech owl's solo whistle
pierces the endless crescendo
of bullfrogs and bumble bees

when Reese at last drifts back out
of evening shadows. He wears
loose flannels. Wrinkled with age,
stained by his long journey,
he still moves with that old grace
over the grass. I see anguish

of long illness on his familiar face
and something like relief too,
that rueful smile, the play finished,

game over. I stand and his arm
settles on my shoulder, a gesture
he used to silence the harrowing
of Jackie Robinson. He helps me
find balance while the world spins
as it always does when I rise
and the whisper of wind is his voice
saying it will be all right, pain is nothing,
stability is overrated, drugs play havoc
with your game, lost sleep only means
waking dreams, and illness is but a high
pop fly that pulls us into shadow.

He is gone as the wind he spoke with
dies down. I find myself on the trail
those deer walked, seeing where I am
now though already lost in a darkness
that soon will reach home.

Winter Solstice

I wake in darkness and fog to the hoofbeat of deer
racing across the hill's frosted crest from east to west.
As in a dream, within the rise and fall of wind I hear
the rise and fall of the deer pack's breath
as it becomes the beat of my heart within my chest.
I am fitted so close to my wife's body her breath
seems to be my breath as we curl together, awake
but not awake, her back rising against my rising chest
in the lingering predawn dark.
Now, in the space between our breath, silence comes to rest.

V.

FROM *THE END OF DREAMS*
(2006)

A Hand of Casino, 1954

My grandfather studies the cards.
His jaw juts and he begins to shift
the pink plate of his false teeth,
tonguing it out and in, mouth
widening till his grin has flipped
upside-down between the gums.
He slams a deuce onto the table.

Even at seven I know he is losing
on purpose. He mumbles deep
in his throat, a gargle of sounds
like someone choking on stones.
I think he would make sense
if his teeth were put in right.

At seven I also know that bodies
crumble but new parts can come
gleaming from dark hiding places.
I have seen, buried at the back
of his top drawer, my father's spare
glass eye in a navy velvet box.

My mother has three heads
of stiff hair inside her closet,
just in case, and a secret pack
of fingernails in her chiffonier.
My grandfather strings phrases
of Polish and Yiddish around words
in French to hold his broken
English together. I understand
nothing he says but everything
that is in his eyes. He tells me
he is *a man from the world.*
That must be where he learned
that losing is winning as a frown

is a smile and a curse is a kiss.
When I lay down the good
deuce, he smacks his furrowed
brow and curses high heaven.

Poolside

There is less than one hour left
and my father does not know.
He lies there in faded light
green trunks, turned belly-up
beneath a livid sunlamp,
chewing his last stick of Dentyne
before the time comes
for him to rise and dress.
He loves the sheer arrogance
of such heat, its dragon's
breath across his chest,
and he fills his lungs with it.

Minutes remain but still
he does not know. He thinks
of the long morning spent
riding bridle paths on a bay
gelding, the midday nap,
pinochle on a sun-drenched
patio and whiskey as clouds
turned his bright day dark
in the blink of an eye.
He thinks of tomorrow only
as a long drive home.

Seconds more as he rises
to stretch and blink salt
from his eyes. He does not
know yet. Without the least
thought of time winding down,
he tucks glasses in a towel
on the lounger and strides
across the deck as though

it were nothing. He breathes,
flexes his toes over the edge,
dives into the cool embrace
of deep water and dies.

Kansas, 1973

My daughter nestled in a plastic seat
is nodding beside me as though in full
agreement with the logic of her dream.
I am glad for her sake the road is straight.
But the dark shimmer of a summer road
where hope and disappointment repeat
themselves all across Kansas like a dull
chorus makes the westward journey seem
itself a dream. She breathes in one great
gulp, taking deep the blazing air, and stops
my heart until she sighs the breath away.
The sun is stuck directly overhead.

I thought it all would never end. The drive,
the heat, my child beside me, the bright day
itself, that fathering time in my life.
We were going nowhere and never would,
as in a dream, or in the space between
time and memory. I saw nothing but sky
beyond the horizon of still treetops
and nothing changing down the road ahead.

Breath

> I weighed about 130 pounds, and I just had to grow a little more.
> I did lots of exercises. I did running and that kind of stuff.
> —Frank Sinatra

For depth of breath young Sinatra
like a boxer ran five morning miles.
Solo on the high school track, thin
as the stripe on a lane, he was all
ears, all bone. He was all business.

The first laps were always for love
songs, nice and easy till he found
his rhythm, drawing the urban air
in deep. The moment he became
one with wind, he knew the way
a body held in check could move
exactly like a melody. It was simple
as swimming underwater. His stride
grew smooth, fingers to shoulders
to hips to toes, graceful as a smile
across low notes as the key shifted.

That was for the long lines of lyric
no one else could hold. In time he ran
for the up-tempo tunes, let go a little
to get the torso involved and bring
his thin arms into play, his gait all glissando.
Step by step he swelled from the inside
out, making himself strong enough
for song. He ran past pain, timed by
the beat of his heart because song
was not about how fast but how long.
This was his Golden Age, Jersey City

in the early Thirties, his moment to make
dreams come true. Music was in the air.
He knew he could go on like that forever
because his dreams began with breath.

O'Connor at Andalusia, 1964

> Sickness before death is a very appropriate thing and I think
> those who don't have it miss one of God's mercies.
> —Flannery O'Connor, *The Habit of Being*

It came with the steady pace of dusk,
slow shadings in the distance, a sense of light
growing soft at the center of her body.
It came like evening to the farm
bearing silence and a promise of rest.
There was nothing to say it was there
till she found herself unable to move
and stillness settled its net over the bed.
A crimson disc of pain suddenly flushed
from her hips like a last flaring of sun.

She believed the time had come
to embrace this perfect weakness
that had no memory of strength,
a mercy even as darkness hardened
inside her joints. It was not to be
missed. Nor was the mercy of sight:
she believed the time had come
to measure every moment and map
the place she soon must leave.
At least she had been given time,
though her wish would have been
an hour more for each leaf visible
from her window, a day for trees,
a week for birds and month to savor
the voice of each friend who called.
Though she never belonged in the heart
of this world, she gave this world her heart.

Within her stillness she remembered
the first signs: that brilliant butterfly
rash on her face, a blink that lasted
for hours, the delicate embrace of sleep
veering as in a dream toward the grip
of death, hunger vanishing like hope.
Her body no longer knew her body as itself

but this too was a mercy. To leave herself
behind and then return was instructive.
To wax and wane, to live beyond
the body and know what that was like,
a gift from God, a mixed blessing shrouded
in the common cloth of loss. Half her life
she practiced death and resurrection.

Whitman Pinch Hits, 1861

After six months of wandering Whitman found himself
at the edge of a Long Island potato farm in early fall.
He saw a squad of young men at sport on sparse grass.
Looking up, he saw a few stray geese rise and circle back
north as though confused by the sudden Indian summer,
then looked down to study cart tracks cut deep into mud.
Weary of his own company, shorn of appetite, he thought
it would be sweet to sit awhile beside this field and watch
the boys in their shabby flannel uniforms playing ball.
Caught between wanting to look at them and wanting
them to look at him, he could not tell from this distance
if the torn and faded blues they wore were soldier's clothes
or baseball clothes. But he loved the rakish tilt of their caps
and cocky chatter drifting on the midday air. He had seen
the game played before, in Brooklyn, on a pebbled patch
laid out beside the sea, and thought it something young,
something brotherly for the frisky young and their brothers
to do in the shadow of civil war. That seemed two lifetimes
ago, not two years. The face he could no longer bear to find
in a mirror looked now like this island's ploughed ground.
Time does turn thick, Whitman thought, does press itself
against a man's body as he moves through a world torn apart
by artillery fire and weeping. Without knowing it happened,

he settled on a rise behind the makeshift home, moving
as he moved all year, a ghost in his own life. He should write
about baseball for the Eagle, or better still, make an epic poem
of it. The diamond chalked on grass, stillness held in a steady
light before the burst of movement, boys with their faces open
to the sky as a struck ball rose toward the all-consuming clouds.
But it was the sound that held him rapt. Wild, musical voices
punctuated by a pock of bat on ball, then the dropped wood
clattering to earth, grunts, everyone in motion through the air,
the resistant air, and then the lovely laughter. Whitman laughed
with them, a soundless gargle. The next batter staggered and fell

drunk, his chin tobacco-splattered, laughing at his own antics
as he limped back to the felled tree where teammates sat.
They shook their heads, ignoring the turned ankle he exposed
for them to admire. Suddenly all eyes turned toward Whitman
where he lounged, propped on one elbow, straw hat tilted
to keep the sun from his neck, on the hill that let him see
everything at once. They beckoned. They needed Whitman
to pinch hit, to keep the game going into its final inning.
The injured batter held his stick out, thick end gripped in his fist,
and barked a curse. Whitman sat up, the watcher summoned
into a scene he has forgotten he did not create. They beckoned
and he came toward them like a bather moving through
thigh-high breakers, time stopping and then turning back,
letting him loose at last amid the spirits that greeted him
as the boys pounded his back, as they turned him around
and shoved him toward the field. In his hands, the wood
felt light. He stood beside the folded coat that represented
home, shifted his weight and stared at the pitcher who glared
back, squinting against the sun, taking the poet's measure.

Latin Lessons

The daughter of the local florist taught
us Latin in the seventh grade. We sat
like hothouse flowers nodding in a mist
of conjugations, declining nouns that
made little sense and adjectives that missed
the point. She was elegant, shapely, taut.
She was dazzling and classic, a perfect
example to us of such absolute
adjectives as *unique* or *ideal* or *perfect*.
The room held light. Suffering from acute
puberty, we could still learn case by case
to translate with her from the ancient tongue
by looking past her body to the chaste
scribblings she left on the board. We were young
but knew that the ablative absolute
was not the last word in being a part
of something while feeling ourselves apart
from everything that mattered most. We chased
each other on the ballfield after class
though it did no good. What we caught was not
what we were after, no matter how fast
we ran. She first got sick in early fall.
A change in her voice, a flicker of pain
across her face, and nothing was the same.
She came back to us pale and more slender
than ever, a phantom orchid in strong
wind, correcting our pronoun and gender
agreement, verb tense, going over all
we had forgotten while she was gone. Long
before she left for good in early spring,
she made sure the dead language would remain
alive inside us like a buried spring.

The End of Dreams

He wakens knowing this to be the day
his hopeless singing voice at last will sound
exactly like the young Robert Goulet.
It is the day for him to touch the ground
as only noble Fred Astaire has done
before, and only once, and with someone

perfect in his arms. He will be able
to accompany himself on the grand
piano by sight, bass hand and treble
hand like swallows in flight, each magic hand
nimble and light as the air that trembles
with the music he will make at the end

of all his dreams. It feels simple and right
to draw in all the air he can, to grow
still, then soar. Now they all stand around
his bed, in tears, and he sees the pure light
that means the time has come for him to sound
the first note, take the first step, and let go.

The Dance

My wife is fiddling "Turkey in the Straw"
in softening summer light. As her feet
begin to shuffle of their own accord,
the air around her softens and the beat
takes hold. Music fills the round room she's in.
It circles her figure, then spirals down
the stairs. As if summoned by her tune, wind
stirs to whirl its way over and around
the lilies blooming in our yard. Swaying
cherry and oak that shade our bed in late
afternoon lose themselves in her playing
too. Now the dance is rippling in one great
wave through the breath of every living thing
here. There is nothing left to do but sing.

The Hermit Thrush

Along the line of dawn a Hermit
Thrush sings down autumn dark.
Breeze stirring oak leaves brings
a sweet odor of hyssop
through our screen and now light
begins to find the room. Eyes shut,
I see the thrush flick its wings
and rusty tail, nervous as the woods
warp around him. Sky shifts in place,
restless with its promise of rain.

You built this house round and snug
to the ground like a nest among
gnarled second growth as if knowing
the time would come for me
to share it. Nothing ever fit me
like the shape of morning here.
I lie still against the curve
of your back as one last dream
produces a trill at the edge
of your breath, its rising phrases
woven into a songbird's spiral.

Eliot in the Afternoon

In the fourth year of drought,
in late September when our parched garden
was lost to spotted spurge and blackberry vine,
when only Russian sage and flannel bush thrived
in their tonsure of blonde grass near our bedroom
window and the fig stood cockeyed with heat,

I sat in a cracked Adirondack chair under twin fir,
occupying the daily zone between analgesic doses,
watching bees traffic around wild rosemary

and saw out of the corner of my eye Eliot show
himself beside our slowly dying well.
                                                     At first
he was pooled light that burst into flame
and became a flare of wind-blown leaves
as I turned to look.
                            Though this light was soaked
up at once by swaying oak and box elder, I had time
to think: You won't need that umbrella here.

I did not remember seeing hallucinations
listed as a side effect of this drug, and with all signs
of him vanished I sat back to catch the frozen
dance of a rufous hummingbird above yarrow.

Then I noticed Eliot's bowler nestled in a fold
of land where we stacked deadfall for winter fires.
I stood, shading my eyes, and saw the hat
for what it was: a dented boulder half emerged
from its niche, our customary seat at the nightly
Concerto for Water Dripping into Near-Empty Tank,
in the key of Despair Minor.
                                      He remained beyond reach,
a shape without mass in the space between trees,

but I knew he had come. All day, to pass the time,
I had been trying to reconcile the cycles
of my illness with the cycles of rainfall, the rise
and fall of temperature or barometer, phases
of moon, patterns of cloud. It seemed fit
that out of such fruitless brooding Eliot should
arrive, accompanied by the warbler's twit twit twit,
and decide not to *come too close.*
                                      I believed it
best to be still, as with a spooked cat, and let
him join all us creatures of the summer heat.

Should I call him Tom or Mr. Eliot?
Should I ask him to sit with me in the shade?
Should I offer him a peach?

I must have slept, because sky was going silver
with vague cirrus when I saw him move across
the gravel drive. He had found a deer trail
that drops toward the creek dry since April
of 1995. But instead of descending, he floated
among the trees as though transformed
to warm breeze.
                      Then he was beside me.

I thought of all the things to avoid mentioning:
the state of poetry today, the fact that I am a Jew,
the mess virus has made of my body or how far
we are from the city. He was an old man
and this was a dry month, season, year. . . .
Best, I thought, not to quote him.
Even better not to amend his lines.

Mr. Eliot, we need to find the deep aquifer.

Especially at summer dusk, we have been lulled by
voices singing out of empty cisterns and exhausted wells.
Lulled by late darkness and the hope of deep mountain
snows next winter, dreams of extravagant melts
next spring followed by long rains that linger
at least through July. Now it is too late, the well
has all but died, only rock and no water
and the gravel road.   Who better to remind us
that the time has come to drill deep, to trace
the remote history of water down so that *time future*
does not *contain time present.*
                              I meant so that cycles
cease to matter because we find ourselves down
where water always flows, the realm of ancient
floodwater freeing us from the desiccated surface
and its arid shallow layers.
                              Tom, we need a new well
and they charge by the foot!
                              For the first time
he turned to smile, the London banker knowing a sound
investment when he heard it. Before I could speak,
he was back where the pooled light had blazed,
afloat as though sailing on a hidden sea. He knew
his way around a small craft and the wind.
He knew his way home without markers.

Soon he began to fade. Or perhaps it was a trick
of light in air too sere to hold him there,
or the presence of my wife, mugs of tea in hand,
smiling at me in a way he only remembered
from late in his life, that second chance at love.

Polite as ever, he took himself to the edge
of the hill, looking down, looking away
over the valley shadowed now by an evergreen,
showing me the light, a shimmering vision
that may have been water, and drifted off.

Dowsing for Joy

The dowser says he can discover joy
as well as water or the whereabouts
of elk in hunting season. Unfurled wire
hangers and forked sticks nestle in a leather
quiver he carries up our gravel drive
until a fold of land calls him to the west.

In the woods he seems half his eighty years
and his pale blue eyes deepen to sapphire
as he gazes where the breeze disappears.
He says there are signs everywhere,
obvious things that most of us simply miss
like the scent of blooming lilies carried on air,
or hidden fields of force that call us home
when we can no longer bear to be alone.
What is music but waves plucked from the sky
and is color not light disturbed before the eye
can find it? He reminds us no one doubts
the fact that wild animals know weather
well enough to hide before a storm arrives.
Are we not animals too? The agitation of a boy
lost in the forest pulls like the moon on tides
if a dowser is tuned in, if he can ask
the right question at the right time and cast
his spirit before him into the dark.

He stops to stake a vein of water for the site
of our well and strings ribbon over limbs
to track its turnings. Something tells him
there is more to know here. Among the oak
and fir he whispers questions to the night
ahead and smiles first at me, then at my wife
as the wires in his fists cross to find us both.

VI.

FROM *THE SNOW'S MUSIC*
(2008)

Georges Braque in Pieces, May 1915

To see the sun shatter before his eyes
is no surprise. To feel the same flaming
shards that pierce clouds also pierce
his skull makes perfect sense to him.
When time stops, when light dissolves,
it all feels familiar. Braque already knows
nothing holds the world in place beyond
the blink of an eye. He knows about broken
contour, a landscape's warped angles
and fractured lines, the truth of God's wild
collage. These have been his life's work.
Braque flails through bloodshot air,
lost in smoke, to settle where the earth's
mouth gapes. Blinded by wounds, he sees
no one and understands when no one sees
him breathing among corpses in this trench
beside the Somme. He cannot move
beneath the weight of so much death.
Stilled, he grasps death as but the final
form life takes, the structure realized
at last, color leached, edges softened,
light only an anticipated memory
before sightless eyes. Then he finds
himself swaddled in a hospital, holes drilled
in his head to release pressure. Cries rise
all around him. The noise is a shade
of foaming cream, is gleaming chrome,
something he has never seen before.
But he remembers it deep in his bones,
the sound of the last moment he was whole.

John Field in Russia, 1835

He has come back to die where darkness lasts.
For days on end he listens to the chant
of frigid winds that seem to circle his bed.
When they pause as if drawing breath,
he hears jingling sleigh bells, and knows
it is an angel's voice lifted in distant song.
A delicate warning made of melody,
all the more ominous for its beauty.
No, not an angel, he does not believe
in angels. It is the snow's own music,
a nocturne heard only in the winter north
when the air is thin enough, when the air
is a broken chord afloat in the night.
Field rises as the wind rises now. He drifts
toward his piano, though the least movement
unleashes a feral animal in his bowels.
Listen, he whispers to lift himself above
the pain, hear the lyrical night. Heed
the passage of time, the mood of looming
darkness stirring like an angel's voice
within the wind. His hands move before
his mind knows the opening theme.

William Butler Yeats among the Ghosts

After seeking them all his life,
Yeats wants only to flee the voices
of ghosts flowing over and around
him now. As the old man rejoiced
at the miracle of his young wife
speaking with the dead, their sound

ragged with anger in her mouth,
so the ageless ghost weeps for want
of a human laugh, a human touch.
The sweet sorrow of lost love taunts
him still, the soft mist of his youth
in the west, the sharp cries and clutch

of hands as he moved through streets
dense with bodies. He misses all
he longed to leave. They are here
but they are one, a great rise and fall
of sound like a wave that never meets
the shore, a vision that never grows clear.

The Young Composers at Play, Westhampton, 1929

Summer heat hangs thick as a curtain.
It keeps everyone else inside the bungalow
discussing jewels and stocks, last year's
failed Broadway productions. But Gershwin
and Rodgers, trailing cigarette smoke,
sweep through, angling toward a stretch
of flat beach where breeze ruffles the sand.

They have known each other only in cramped
apartments or theaters, jockeying for position
at a grand piano in someone's living room,
passing with handshakes on the city's streets.
But now they hop and banter about burning
feet, move through a chorus of seagulls,
come to a stop where old sandals mark
a makeshift court. They drop their racquets,
squat to measure slope, scuff a sharp
new set of boundary lines. Gershwin rolls
his trouser cuffs, chattering against a foamy
hiss of breakers. Rodgers flips the shuttlecock
from hand to hand, humming a melody
the sun softens, something his friend snatches
in a heartbeat and turns back on itself.

Moving together, still carrying the tune
between them, they raise and plant the poles,
slap the net free of seaweed, and begin
to volley in the heavy air. Silent now,
stiff in their movements, they fail to find
a rhythm for their game. Each feather
of the shuttlecock is visible as it spins
within a bleached blue light, each thread
holding them in place sparkles, each swish
and pock of a swing declares itself as separate
sound. Then Gershwin grabs the shuttlecock

and brings play to a halt. He wipes his brow
and smiles, taps his foot, nods in time,
and looks to see Rodgers nodding back,
rising on his toes to receive the serve.

Balance

The ear that hears wind chatter in cedar
woods listens also to the earth curve
beneath your feet. It holds you in place
as you move through a spinning world.
Look up in mid-June and see the icy
anvil of cumulonimbus drift, look down
and see a storm forecast in clumps
of velvetgrass, look ahead at ruffles
along a colt's mane: motion within
motion with only a maze of hair cells
to keep you steady, reading what eye
and skin notice. Now the deerbrush
dances where a swallowtail lands.
Now your wife's breath touches
your cheek in passing as you walk
uphill together, leaning into the steep
slope that years seem to lengthen,
and from the corner of your eye comes
a zigzag flash of blue wing. It leaves
behind a soft song, equal parts fear
and delight, that is almost sweet
enough to knock you off your feet.

First Light, Late Winter

If you live deep enough within the heart
of woods, and wake just as the long night
begins loosening its grip on first light
and birdsong, you never know what might dart
across the fading screen of dreams.
This is the time when memory
is feral. Your eyes remain closed to see
your brother live again, then open to evergreen
shapes looming outside your window
that become your brother petrified
with terror at the moment death pried
him loose. You think you know
where you are but are lost for good,
at home at last within the heart of woods.

Transformations

The molecules in my brain
are no longer the same
as the ones that first knew
your smile, but the memory
of that moment remains.
My new skin remembers
your first touch, my reborn
heart the first steady beats
of yours against my chest.
The small oval window
in the wall of my ear,
where nothing is the way
it was then, still holds the sound
of your first sleeping breath.

Silent Music

My wife wears headphones as she plays
Chopin études in the winter light.
Singing random notes, she sways
in and out of shadow while night
settles. The keys she presses make a soft
clack, the bench creaks when her weight shifts,
golden cotton fabric ripples across
her shoulders, and the sustain pedal clicks.
This is the hidden melody I know
so well, her body finding harmony in
the give and take of motion, her lyric
grace of gesture measured against a slow
fall of darkness. Now stillness descends
to signal the end of her silent music.

Ezra Pound in a Spring Storm

Amity, Oregon, 2006

The night we sold our house a storm blew in
from the Coast Range, whirling as if enraged
by what we had done. I saw lights vanish
from the valley below, heard the woods hiss
around us in the first drizzle, and a pack of deer
rush east across the hill's crest to flee a volley
of hail. In a lull between squalls, drenched oak
like wild horses shook rain from their leaves,
bearded iris thrashed in a swirl of crosswind
beneath my window, and keening sounds rose
from within the woods that I first took to be cries
from the heart of the land itself. Why not?
After fourteen years here, I thought nothing
would surprise me.
                    But then in a sudden shaft
of moonlight, cursing as he lurched over slick
leaves and steadied himself with a moss-covered
maple branch, Pound made his way upslope
from a thicket of blackberry vines. Beard biblical,
voice blazing, he stopped to glare at me.
How could'st thou leave thy cottage in the woods?

I knew there would be inspectors testing water
and septic, roof and foundation, but Pound
probing my mind had never crossed my mind.

Would he care that aging parents drew us back
to the city, or that the time had come for younger
bodies to tend this land?
                          I saw he was lost
in memory, mourning his days with Yeats,
their cottage in the woods. Gone forever,
he had written in a fit of nostalgia. Yet not.

As I reached for him, Pound raised his branch,
or perhaps the giant fir looming above him
swayed as he spoke, and it was the voice
of the mad prophet from his late Cantos.
What thou lovest well is thy true heritage.

The glow he dwelt in faded with a shift of wind
and I saw him swallowed by his own shadow.
No, by his cape flung across his face
as he drew nearer, hair ruffling like a mane.
I had time only to tell him I would never leave
this place no matter where I lived.
But he was already all motion, a storm
departing, deaf to everything.
                                      Backed by
distant thunder, his voice was a flicker
of lightning all around me. Then came
stillness I would take with me everywhere.

Digging Zak's Grave

These hands crusted with dark
red soil have reached back
seven million years in a stroke
of spade. They also touch
yesterday's fallen leaves,
the mulch from a dozen years
of fruits and vegetables,
and this afternoon's loss.
Time means nothing we can
grasp until it is converted
to memory. Now, drenched
in sweat, I am stained by
what remains of Columbia River
lavas that covered this hill
in Miocene times. If rain
and snow can do such slow
work on rock, they will have no
trouble with the body I am
about to consign to this hole.

VII.

FROM *CLOSE READING*
(2014)

Jules Verne above Amiens, 1873

All night Verne visits the balloon
in his mind. Sleep is a dream lost
within the long dream of flight soon
to be real, and time stands still
within the moon-drenched room,
within the envelope of bedsheet
now grown too heavy to be tossed
aside. After all these years! He tries
to forget the balloon is out there,
tethered to the ground in the square
he can almost see in shadows beside
his house. Yearning to rise, teased
by the midnight summer breeze,
waiting for the light of dawn to flare.

*

At first there is too much to see
and feel as he drifts above trees
reddened in the first autumn chill.
He shivers and wonders why
he failed to consider how the soul
might vibrate in such pure air.

The gondola sways when he moves
to follow the Somme bending south,
turns back to catch sunlight flash
off the cathedral dome, leans out
to watch a small boat nudge its way
through marsh, the morning train
shrink as it speeds toward Paris.

He tries to think about issues of lift
and ballast, heat and current, forces
himself to gaze at the barometer

and note its fall. If his calculations
are correct, the sea will soon be
a glimmer in the west. Ambient air
weighs more than . . . But he finds
himself laughing at the sight of birds
scattering as he passes among them.
Looking up, he sees thin clouds
ripple like an echo of the wind.

    *

What he had written of flight before
was drawn from imagination fired
by long study. The extraordinary
voyages of a boy longing for the sea,
polar ice, a glimpse into the earth's
molten core. Of course the whole
fabric of his fiction is thin as the skin
now holding him aloft, but it fills him
with pleasure to feel in his body
how much he has gotten right.

He must take notes. *Transported
to a world of dreams.* He knows
the air is not quite a slow river
but yet he soars as hidden currents
shift, and almost loses his grip.
How could a man not see before
he dies what it is to be free
of the land, to live even for an hour
where his kind cannot live?
Oh, and the sudden uplift is just
as he described it, remembering

his first moments on the water
as a child. With the sun behind him,
Verne looks down into the heart
of Amiens, searching for his home.

Paul Klee at Sixty

Slowly the stillness comes upon his hand.
As he watches, color bleeds from the tip
of his brush, leaving him only a thick
black line. He has dreamt it time and again
but this is no dream. He knows he is sick
beyond all imagining now. A land
of loss looms, and is the place he must walk
this tired line, which thins as it wavers
toward the vanishing point. He cannot rest.
As his skin shrinks, as his muscles soften,
what he most wants to bring to life is death
as it looks to him here, pure fire often
blazing in the coldest place. He savors
it as he waits for movement to begin.

The Shared Room

My brother was a Brylcreemed pompadour
and my brother was rock 'n' roll first thing
every morning. Then he was a four-door
Valiant, smoldering Kent, star-sapphire ring
on the pinky. He was small savvy smiles
and a wink, a deck of cards, shiny suit,
shot cuffs, Windsor knots. My brother was miles
ahead. He was goodbye, a man en route.
I was another story. I was crew
cut and tucked shirt, double-knotted shoes, please
and thank you. I was too small to hit, too
big for my britches. Cracker Barrel cheese
instead of Velveeta. Sorry, not Clue.
Cute, not suave, and too dumb to be believed.

Nostrand Avenue

Brooklyn, 1955

I remember the street was full of noise,
trolleys screeching and sizzling under
sparking wires, taxis honking as braying boys
dashed past and cellar doors thundered shut.
It was autumn and I wanted to hear leaves fall.
My mother's words were air and cigarette
smoke rising toward the clear sky. A bus
gushed to a stop and there were more people
before us, forcing us to stop. I saw a man
dance and flap around the corner to find
a woman holding out her hands to join him.
They whirled, blinded to everything around them
as they laughed and cried. People leaned to cheer
from cars, doorways, windows, rooftops.
A butcher waved his cleaver. A priest wept.
Then a flash of sunlight off a windshield,
and the brush of my mother's overcoat
as she pulled me into the ordinary afternoon
light, fading now like the last note of a song.
No matter how hard I try, this is always
where the memory stops, before I come to
understand the Dodgers have won at last.

My Grandparents' Dance

My grandparents' stately polka was done
in waltz time no matter the music's speed.
They turned slow whistling circles that spun
through other dancers' wakes and freed
something in them I had never seen before.
This smiling man was the old-country Max,
so graceful as he moved across the floor
with a hand spread low on Rose's back,
and this gliding woman with fingertips
grazing Max's shoulder flowed on the rise
and fall of their dance as she slipped
the weight of all her years, head back, eyes
closed. Her gown sparkled as she twirled under
his raised arm and he gazed down in wonder.

The Shore

The old men belching up their lunches
take hard rolls from coat pockets,
sit on boardwalk benches, and sigh.
They toss scraps to circling seagulls,
sparing no words for the tumbling surf,
having nothing to say about sunlight
streaming through a break in clouds
right above their heads. It is enough
to frown at one another, brows raised,
and flutter their fingers, which means
don't worry, things will get worse soon,
because by now they all know this God.
So they kvetch about the nursing home's
soups, cream of kohlrabi, cream of carrot,
cream of beet. Enough with the roots,
already! And corn on the cob when no
one has real teeth, chicken cooked since
the end of World War II, crumbling rolls
even a bird spits out. They nearly smile,
warming up, coughing into their hands.
Never such food, not in the old country
when crops failed, not all those winter
months in the woods, or in the hospital
with the gall bladder. Now they nod
and fall silent. My grandfather, sinking
toward sleep, lets the last crumbs scatter.

Close Reading

for Thomas Kinsella

The sun sank behind us as we drove past
Crab Orchard Lake in my battered Falcon.
It coughed and rattled at forty but we spoke
above the noise, three young poets eager
for our evening's close reading with the master.
"Fern Hill" was about the lost childhood Eden!
"Fern Hill" was about death! About time!
All poems were about Death and Time!

In his formal dining room, Kinsella placed
us at the table like poker players beneath
a blazing chandelier. We spread the text
and bent to our task. Then he asked why
the poem began with *Now* and brought
all pronouncements to a sudden stop.

*

Gerry sat in an oak rocker, dangling one
last ornament for his Christmas tree.
Bob and I stood across the small room,
ready with advice. The doorbell rang.
Kinsella entered, gloved, hatted, stamping
snow from his boots, streaming vapor
as he spoke, helping Eleanor remove
her coat. We shook his hand and asked
where he thought the ornament should go.
He studied Gerry's tree, blinked at its blinking
lights, said things were perfect as they were:
Anything more would just be for effect.

*

At forty-one he seemed correct and neat
as a sonnet. The thick beard trimmed, hair flat
across his scalp, voice clear, words precise, feet
on the floor like a couplet when he sat.
But there was something radical going
on beneath the surface. Order opposed
by sheer formlessness in new work growing
stranger as he turned inward. I supposed
he would teach me how to write poems clean
and tight as he used to write them, verse strict
as he looked. That he would reveal to me
the secret of where poems came from. He
would show me the hidden ways to inflict
form, and what being a poet might mean.

*

Instead, we practiced close reading.
Who is speaking in the second stanza?
We scoured excess, awkward statement,
clotted imagery, extreme verbal gesture,
slackness, the least readiness to settle
for the rhetorical. *See here, a bee
cannot repeatedly sting. This is false.*
We followed the management of data
in every poem, found the order it sought
to establish. *What's a foot doing here?*
Nothing should stand between the poet
and the thing perceived. *Montague
does not encrust his verse irrelevantly.*

At winter's end, Gerry, Bob, and I stopped
to buy a fifth of Jameson and handed it
to Kinsella when he opened the door.
He read the label, almost smiled, and set

the bottle down on a credenza. Saying
we'll address this later, he led us to
the dining table where the light never wavered.

	*

Our poems were read in the living room,
not the dining room. We sat in a loose
arc of easy chairs, subjecting the work
to *a primary appreciation.* One night
a month to us, three nights to Eliot,
Pound, Murphy. He would call one
of our names, nod in the chosen poet's
direction, lift the paper into the light
of his reading lamp, and direct
his avid glance to our words.

	*

At seventy-nine, his voice on the disc
is still deep and direct. He reads his work
as you would expect, the tone sharp, pace brisk.
Nothing wasted, no frills. If shadows lurk,
they lurk where they should, in the poems' dark
depths brought to light by his words. I will hear
this voice to the end of my days, the stark
truth of it over time, helping me clear
my own way toward what I need to say.

Isaac Bashevis Singer in the Reading Room, 1968

This old man in the armchair's plush embrace
waits for his thoughts to settle. He is not
my grandfather despite the wrinkled face,
gleaming skull, vast snout, gargly voice, and odd
twist of lips. They sound like men from the same
village in an old country bordering
on nowhere to be found again. He takes
a deep breath and shifts his weight, ordering
familiar words he has brought together
to address the final question of the night:
You see, I'm only a storyteller,
not a psychologizer. I just write
a beginning, a middle, and an end.
The meaning I leave to you, my good friend.

In Thompson Woods with John Gardner, 1970

He shuffled through my poems as we walked
along the trail. Falling hickory leaves grazed
his hair. He slapped the pages when he talked.
"Never use the word *tremble*." The path, glazed
with morning rain, crossed a patch of sunlight
and his face turned a moment toward the sky.
"Don't use *awe*, either, but feel it." To our right
as the wind rose, oak limbs bowed in a shy
curtsy. "And call things by their proper names."
He stopped to light his pipe and explain why
everyone should write at least one epic,
as he was doing, because the lyric
was a romantic trap. He closed one eye.
"Remember, art's not just fun and games."

Sway

I lie back on the narrow bed
and do not know what to do
with my hands. A woman
looms above me, fitting two
chocks tight against my head,
and warns me yet again
not to move. Earphones hiss.
I close my eyes before
beginning to slip
into the magnet's bore.
Soon I hear faint music play
beneath the MRI's
jackhammer rattle. "Sway,"
by Dean Martin, and I
feel its mambo rhythm take
hold down through my toes.
It is all I can do to make
them be still as Dino's
soused-sounding baritone
fills my brain. I need to sing
along now. I have known
this song, from the first *bing
bing* of the chorus to the last
mellow *now*, since learning
the lyrics as a boy whose vast
fantasies included turning
himself into a crooner. I am
in a bath of sense, memory,
and dye. My brain scan
must be lit up like a night sky
by the northern lights. But no,
it is not that kind of test,
and then the music stops so
I can hear that the next

phase will last fifteen
minutes, that I have done
very well so far, and please
remember to be still again.

Painted Lady

My wife stands among the drumstick
allium at her garden's eastern border.
Camera poised in late afternoon light,
she waits as a painted lady circles,
lands on the deep scarlet flower,
then flies off when a honeybee climbs
beside it like a weary mountaineer.
No breeze, no clouds, and now I see
I am not even breathing as she holds
still, watching, whispering to the air.
The butterfly returns, comes to rest,
and slowly opens its brilliant wings.

At Rowan Oak

Oxford, Mississippi

Faulkner is nowhere and everywhere
here, adrift among oak grown thick
with all the years he has been gone.
Scent of magnolia sweetens the air.
Shadows litter the portico as we walk
the alley of cedars. Summer heat rises
to shimmer between us and the white
clapboard home that keeps him still
for us in time. Inside, an office wall
is covered with the outline of *A Fable*.
A small table holds his old Underwood.
My daughter, freshly finished writing
her first book, leans across the threshold.

VIII.

FROM *APPROACHING WINTER*

(2015)

My Grandfather's Final Day in the Old Country, 1892

Last night soldiers on horseback circled
the house of worship. He saw the blazing
roof cave in, heard screams, felt heat curl
around his body, but thought it all a crazy
dream. Would God let His own house be consumed
in fire? Now charred wood and ash coat the mud,
the lungs, lingering in air near the ruined
synagogue. Glass shards catch the morning sun.
God allows the holy ark to burn? At twelve
he already knows what the Rabbi would say
to that question, if the Rabbi were still alive:
Evidently, my child. This is the day
he should be walking his brother to school
for the first time, but the school is cinder
and thin spirals of smoke. If it were true,
as the Rabbi taught, that God's fire bore
the light from which the universe was formed,
could it be that fire was not such a bad thing?
What is God saying when He brings harm
to bear upon people gathered to sing
His praises, and then lets the very place
where they sing dissolve in flame? He has seen
what he came to see, so he turns to face
the river one last time, closes his eyes, breathes
in the unfamiliar air, and tries to pray.

October 30, 1938

    The night Martians landed in New Jersey
    my father was just across the Hudson River
    asking for my mother's hand in marriage.
    My grandfather is supposed to have said
    You can have all of her. Then they drank
    a schnapps, toasting life, toasting my mother
    pacing in another room, and sat on the sofa
    listening to chaos rising from the street.

    It was a Sunday, getting late, getting dark,
    and all my father could think about was
    why such traffic? He had to be awake
    by four, open his market by five, it was
    already late to be driving back to Brooklyn.

    As he stood, someone cried out on the fire
    escape above. A radio crackled with static
    as the wind shifted and rose, making scraps
    of newspaper drift past the window.
    He thought about all my mother wanted—
    the honeymoon in Cuba, aproned maid,
    ritzy apartment on a top floor, his thick
    hands washed clean of blood *even
    under the fingernails* before he ever
    entered their home—and knew himself to be
    in an alien world. But he was thirty,
    she was twenty-eight, and it was time.

    He walked out into the cold and saw
    on a stoop across the street a woman
    wearing ragged slippers and a mink stole
    kneeling in prayer as the crowd rushed east.
    One carried a canary in its cage.
    A man grabbed my father's arm. *It's happening*

right now! Tears streaked the man's face
as he said, *They've got heat rays and poison
gas. You'll never make it* and my father thought
But I just did. His car was surrounded,
a couple in evening wear draped across
its hood, a child perched on its rear bumper
holding a stuffed platypus. *The Martians
are big as skyscrapers and fast as express
trains. Jersey's gone. They're coming this way.*

My father unlocked the door and looked
back a moment to see my mother framed
in her window, face turned away from him
as she watched her neighbors flowing
out of sight. He knew it was going to take
all night to find his slow way home.

Dream of a Childhood

Childhood was a raft drifting across
the Pacific. It was sometimes a shiny yellow
Geiger counter and sometimes the polio
vaccine at last, which meant you could swim
again in public pools. Childhood was a fat
stack of Green Stamp books on a cloverleaf
table in the foyer. It was coonskin caps
on boys from Brooklyn, then the end of *Wait
Till Next Year*. All you had to do was dream.
Waking to "Yakety Yak" on the radio,
moving so fast no one heard it but you,
childhood was don't turn on the lights,
tiptoe around the kitchen so your mother
continued sleeping. It was a week's worth
of hard-boiled eggs peeled and waiting
in the refrigerator. It was your mother's dream
of no mess, no trace, no mornings to endure.
Childhood was grade school beside a Nike
missile base on the bay side of a barrier
island. It was duck-and-cover drills in home
room. Teachers had ham radios and decals
from all forty-eight states, foreign coins
in a plate on the desk. One called you Dream
Boat when you gazed out the winter window
and began to doze. Teachers ate lunches
in a secret room stacked with Tupperware
and recalled honeymoons dancing in Havana.
Brothers drove Tango Red Chryslers
to land's end and back, over and over.
You dreamed yours would be Parisian Blue
and go twice as fast as his. Sisters had packs
of Old Gold cigarettes you saw dancing in ads
on television. Friends' mothers wore frilled
aprons. They carried platters of standing
rib roast, fixed molded domes of lemon Jell-O

mixed with tomato sauce and topped by loops
of mayonnaise. Fathers rose in the dark
and vanished till the dark returned them
ready for sleep, ready for their own dreaming.

Handspun

My wife sits in her swivel chair
ringed by skeins of multicolored yarn
that will become the summer sweater
she has imagined since September.
Her hand rests on the spinning wheel
and her foot pauses on the pedals
as she gazes out into the swollen river.
Light larking between wind and current
will be in this sweater. So will a shade
of red she saw when the sun went down.
When she is at her wheel, time moves
like the tune I almost recognize now
that she begins to hum it, a lulling
melody born from the draft of fiber,
clack of spindle and bobbin, soft
breath as the rhythm takes hold.

Approaching Winter

Late afternoons when the sun slips behind
the hills I like to sit by my window
facing east and watch shadows capture
the river. Cormorants skim the surface
as though preying on the edge of light
and yellow tugboats nudge gravel barges
into the spreading dark. Once I saw a siege
of herons packed onto the trunk of a young
ash tree swirling in current after a storm.
Now a kayak gliding downstream vanishes
as it follows the bank's curve below me.
In a few months I'll be sixty-five.

Lately, at this time of day, I'm not
always sure where the borders of sleep
might be. Memory ebbs and floods as I try
not to doze. My infant daughter's voice
is somewhere within the calls of circling
eagles though she is two thousand miles
away, a grown woman at work on a book
in her own attic aerie. My father smiles
and dives into a pool where he is about
to die, but surfaces in front of me here,
playful as an otter in these waters.
My wife stands near me at her easel
breaking the river into bold vectors
of color. Her sweet alto rises
with the tune flowing into her ears.

As I stare, a shift in wind transforms
the midriver pattern into prairie
grass, into ice losing hold of itself,
then into Hemingway on a paddleboard
waving at me. He wants me to move,
I think, wants to lure me out of the house

and onto the fishing boat he must command,
anchored near the pilings where a dock
used to be. Across the river, at the tip
of Ross Island where cottonwoods are still
holding their leaves, an overturned stump
can only be Gertrude Stein signaling
with a flutter of arms that she expects
to join us. We'll need to avoid Moses
in his cradle now drifting close to shore
disguised as the bole of a white oak.

The room has grown cold. When my wife lights
the fire behind me, the window fills
with its flickering glow. It's a kind of smile
that eases me from the chair, and she's there
with me, both ready for the night to come.

Crying over "Scarlet Ribbons"

I remember my daughter wanted pink
plastic barrettes for her hair. One on each
side of her forehead. They are there, I think,
in this blurred photo of her on a beach
somewhere in Washington, and in this one,
sitting on a ceramic pirate's lap
at a zoo in Madison, Wisconsin.
I swear they are under her sailor cap
here as she drives a tiny British race car
in Tomorrowland. On a camping trip
through North Dakota, one beloved star-
shaped barrette was lost when I failed to clip
it properly in place. We backtracked all
the way to Grand Forks in search of new
pink stars. And here she stands in early fall,
hair grown longer now, light finding the two
barrettes we bought at an old drug store just
as the day and our hopes seemed lost.

Today

Johnny is John now, and Billy is Bill.
Though I haven't seen them in fifty years
it feels like we're boys together still.
When his voice breaks, John's boyhood face appears
across the miles, and when Bill speaks of storms
we survived on our barrier island home
I forget and call him Billy, which makes
John gasp because it hurts so much to laugh.
The cancer has come back. He says it takes
all his strength some mornings just to take half
a breath, but then there might be a whole day
when he can almost forget, like today.

Dylan Thomas at Sundown, November 9, 1953

Dylan Thomas drifts above the sea,
savoring the sundown light of memory.
Waves lap the shingle. He feels nothing
beneath his empty body and decides
he must be riding a froth of cloud.

What surprises him most is the pure
silence within and without. It folds
over itself like the breakers below.
He thought there would be music
at the end, something like the melody
of starburst, and singing, flowing lyrics
in a language known only to angels.
He thought there would be nothing
like time, nothing like this sense of loss.

Afloat on dead air, he sees himself
sprint across hay fields. Thirty years
gone in the blink of an eye. He is far
ahead of the children chasing with voices
fading. Not even the desperate fox
can keep pace as the wild boy flashes by.
He always knew this would be the moment
remembered forever. Life was one mad
dash to a finish line hidden at land's end,
a quick lick. He would be breathless
at the end, down on his knees as if in prayer,
but finally able to slow his heart, his mind,
there at the darkening ocean's edge.

Samuel Beckett Throws Out the First Pitch

Ebbets Field, Brooklyn, August 1957

The lanky lefty standing on the first-base
side of the mound flips the ball from hand
to hand and studies the distance between
late afternoon shadow and evening light.

No one is sure who he is. The former cricket
bowler S. B. Beckett, his letter had said.
Irish, long retired from the sport, and that
was good enough for the O'Malley family
to welcome him in the melancholy dog
days of their Dodgers' last season in Brooklyn.

Friends imagine him in London or Paris,
maybe somewhere in Normandy, out of touch,
at work on a play. But he imagines himself
in a place where play as he'd known it
at last becomes strange enough for joy.
He has dressed in white from shoes to jumper.

Under his fierce stare home plate transforms
itself into a wicket right before the bored
eyes of Roy Campanella settling into a crouch
and expecting a soft lob from an old man
about to vanish from sight. Then the ball
in Beckett's huge hand turns red as he molds
his fingers against its crease. He squares up.

All around him are the ruins of a great
stadium and he sees what will become of it,
smashed to rubble and broken memory,
names echoing in thickened air. Now ghosts
drift in a warp of time like the voices

of this sparse crowd paying no attention
as Beckett sinks deeper into himself.

He calls to mind the form of a perfect pitch,
the spin ball he will unleash from a windmilling
arm, the held breath filled with nothing but his own
heartbeat, a silent moment before action
that he never wants to end. Then, stifling a cry,
he begins to run straight toward home.

Sightings

I saw my brother in the sunstruck glass
of a nearby high-rise on the September
morning he would have turned seventy-two.
It was as though he had escaped the past
and all I could no longer remember.
I knew he was that flash of reflected light,
dazzling with life, in the same way I knew
he was the sudden gust of wind last night
that woke me as it spoke of things he did
not live to do. The waning summer moon
snagged in the river was him till he hid
from me behind the cloud that soon
gathered what glow remained. Wind-borne
songs he never heard reach me here,
dense with echoes of his raw baritone,
warmer than ever, unforgettably clear.

Lost in the Memory Palace

I found my brother in the attic
of the memory palace
hunched over our old Silvertone
under rafters where late afternoon
light streamed through a gable vent.
His face wavered in a haze of dust.
Before I could speak he looked
up and raised a finger to his lips.
The sound of wind was the soft
southern voice of Red Barber
broadcasting a Dodgers game.
Ol' Duke's easy as a bank of fog.

It wasn't supposed to work
like this. I should know where I've put
people to find them in a heartbeat:
Father buried long ago in the cellar,
mother at the piano in the parlor,
brother eating Velveeta before
the open fridge. But then
just this morning—I think it was
this morning—my father stumbled out
of the library where he would never
be found. He had a book in hand,
the title concealed by his fingers,
and was smiling in a way I never saw
him smile before. I almost missed him,
thinking the short man with the bald
spot gleaming as he turned must be me.

I don't remember my brother
doing anything like that scene in the attic.
No secret corners of rooms, no hunching

over radios, no hushed moments I recall.
He filled his spaces, and was gone
whenever I couldn't hear or see him.

And now I don't know where
my mother is because she seems to be
everywhere at once. I can hear her
in the parlor playing the opening chords
of "Bewitched, Bothered and Bewildered,"
but instead of singing she screams
from the living room where a smudged
fingerprint has been found on a low
credenza we never owned.

She also waits at the bottom of the ladder
I used to climb into the attic, arms
akimbo, smoke from her Chesterfield
drifting up to mingle with the dust.

Thomas Hardy in the Dorset County Museum

Turned sideways in a desk chair,
elbow perched on its top rail,
the life-size cardboard Thomas Hardy
looks wary. Even when no one is here
Hardy sits tight, certain something
must take him from happy solitude.
Work is everywhere now, a poem's
lines whirling in a figure eight above
his head, chapter one of a novel
looming behind him, rough drafts
of letters under glass at his knee.
Apologizing, knowing he never liked
being touched, I drape my arm over
his shoulder as my wife takes our picture.
He is much younger than I am,
not the sage Hardy with wizened face,
wispy hair and waxed mustache tips.
His beard is darker, thicker, his hair
shorter, but the matching domes
of our foreheads are enough to
let me feel what I have come all
this way to feel. It is time to move on
to the place where he was born.

IX.

FROM *FAR WEST*
(2019)

The Lost Name

One day this fall I could not remember
the name of the island in Hawaii
where we'd spent a week in December.
There was a wall around the word.

I closed my eyes. Then I thought
of the red-crested cardinal who kept
returning to our lanai, the yellow tang
ablaze in the reef as sunlight swept

through a quick break of cloud, the sprawling
banyan tree near Lahaina Harbor. Names
everywhere in my brain, nerve cells sparkling
with names. Crimson opakapaka came

to mind. Haleakalā. Snorkel Bob's.
But not the island. Not the sound
of it, not even the first letter. If I let
go, thought of something else, looked around,

it might come to me. I knew I could open
Rand McNally, check online, ask my wife.
Green turtles and breaching humpback whales.
Cattle egret glimpsed in the blink of an eye.

Tangled

He's that actor you don't remember
from the movie you've seen a dozen times
or more. In the background, maybe "September
Song" but you can't be sure. Was he in the scene
on an island drenched in reds and green,
angles widening as morning sun climbs
above the trees and in a heartbeat fades
into mist? He has the soft voice you hear
only later, outside, sounding the way blades
of grass look to you when autumn skies clear.
What was it he whispered? All that remains
is the whisper itself tangled in notes
from some other song. Its melody floats
now just beyond the sound made by two skeins
of Canada geese coming together,
gathering to face the heavy weather.

Over and Over

My brain is a jukebox stuffed with old songs
playing a phrase or two at random over
and over. I keep the volume turned low
but you can sometimes see my lips move
as I sing along, eyebrows rising as I reach
for a silent high note. If you asked me
whether I know the lyrics to "Over and Over"
I would say *No* and blame it on being
past seventy, then find the song
repeating in my head an hour later as I fold
the laundry. Bobby Day, 1958, B-side
of "Rockin' Robin." I'm eleven and listening
to my brother's 45s before he gets home
from school. *I went to a dance the other night.*
Everybody went stag. Also late 1965,
The Dave Clark Five. *I said over and over*
and over again this dance is gonna be
a drag. I'll hear both versions off and on
for hours till someone says *wasn't it awful*
about the tanker fire yesterday morning?
and then I'll hear the soft piano and drums
opening into "Smoke Gets In Your Eyes."
They asked me how I knew. I don't know
how I still know these lyrics. Haven't thought
of them in fifty years at least. The Platters,
Nat King Cole, Eartha Kitt. Just a boy.
But now the lines repeat and expand, melody
and rhyme tricky, *When your heart's on fire,*
you must realize, all the way to dinnertime
when I start preparing trout with lime, cilantro,
and coconut. That unleashes Harry Nilsson
singing *put the lime in the coconut,* the only
phrase I know from his song. I'm not even sure

I've heard "Coconut" from beginning to end
but those six words repeat over and over
till now, just thinking *over and over* again,
there it is: *I went to a dance the other night.*

Jet Song

West Side Story, August 1962

As soon as we were sure we knew the dance
the choreographer changed it. Instead
of jumping onto the bench from stage left,
leap over it from behind. Can you lift
your arms as you land? Riff and A-rab, thread
your way through that line of trash bins, and glance
at each other when you sing the word *Jet*.
Let's have you start to spin on *cigarette*.
I can hear her smoke-scorched voice even now
urging us to reach for the sky on our last
dying day. Move as one. You are a gang!
In the echoing space the mirrored room sang
our songs back on us. Don't twirl, try a fast
fan kick and when you hunch and snap, stay low.
Forget the very idea of steps but be
sure you remember the steps themselves—free
yourselves to move the music among you
so your bodies contain the whole story
in each step, and the dancing will be true.

Chris Cagle Is Dead

1955

I spread my old-time All-American
football cards in T-formation
on my parents' bedroom floor as they dress
for dinner with friends.
Now playing quarterback:
Little Frankie Albert!
He throws a pass into the hall
where Bill Daddio makes a leaping catch
and laterals to Choo-Choo Charlie Justice
by the antique chest of drawers!

I love to say the players' names
and sometimes if he's in a good mood
ask my father what they do now.
He always knows.
Whizzer White is a lawyer
and *Johnny Lujack sells Chevys.*
Beattie Feathers is a coach down south.
Cotton Warburton makes movies in Hollywood.

But tonight my father paces while he ties
and re-ties his Windsor knot,
no longer even speaking to my mother
about how late
she will make them again.
He stops long enough to find
his cufflinks, rattles them like dice in his palm.

My mother lights
another Chesterfield and glares
at him in her mirror. So I begin
picking up my cards.
As my father passes, I reach out

to show him my new favorite.
He slaps it to the floor.
Chris Cagle is dead.

    *

1929

The back of his card says he was a bolt
of lightning: Fast, dangerous, Army's best
broken-field runner ever. Nicknamed *Red*,
the fiery Cagle thought a helmet slowed
him down. If he had to wear one, he kept
the chin strap loose. Loved to hit and be hit.

    *

1961

I still don't know where I am.
I still don't know what happened
but my brother says he'll give me
another concussion if I ask again.

It's dark and he's in his bed
watching *Have Gun—Will Travel*.
I can't imagine how
it could be Saturday night.

My head hurts.
There's a scab forming on my lower lip
in the shape of my upper teeth.
There are too many pillows on my bed.

The last thing I remember
is returning to the school bus

because we'd come to the wrong field.
No marching band, no fans, no opponents.
I shuffle among my teammates in our dark-
blue uniforms, wind whishing through
my helmet's ear holes, cleats clattering
across the blacktop. Then the bus starts

and I wake up in my bed
across the room from my brother
unable to decide if the sound
of gunfire comes from the television
or inside my head. My brother looks
at me, sighs and agrees
to tell me what happened
one last time.

He says I took a hard hit to the head
returning the opening kickoff
and later in the quarter made open
field tackles on four straight plays.
From the bleachers he could see
I was woozier after each play,
staggering back to my position, shaking
my head. He was making his way
down to alert the coach
as the fifth play began.
He says he vaulted the fence
and ran to me. He says he covered
my convulsing body with his.

*

1963

I sit on a bench in the locker room
wrapping my ankles in tape.
Then I step into a girdle of hip
and tailbone pads, lacing them tight.
I slip thigh and knee pads into slots
on my pants, then reach my arms
through straps on shoulder pads,
and adjust a pair of elbow pads.
I put on my helmet, snap the chin strap,
adjust the face mask, stuff a mouth guard
in place. Beside me, my best friend
Jay slaps the sides and top of my helmet
bing bang boom and we walk
toward Saturday morning light
funneling through the field house doors.

I remember the whistle blew the play dead.
I remember stopping beside a pile
of players at midfield and then I remember
waking up on the ground without feeling
in my fingers or toes. I wanted to get up.
The referee began blowing his whistle again,
screaming *late hit late hit* as he threw down
a penalty flag and Jay knelt beside me.
I remember his helmet coming into view,
black stripes under his eyes and his voice
telling me not to move.

My mother said *If your father were alive
to see this again.* She said *that first time
he had nightmares you'd be a vegetable
the rest of your life, God forbid.* She didn't say

I killed him with worry but she might as well.
You, young man, are lucky to be alive.

Next year, she tore up the permission form.
No more football! I spent that season
working in a butcher's freezer cutting beef
and pork I'd hauled from delivery trucks,
pretending I was tackling them for a loss.

    *

1942

The night after Christmas, two men found
Cagle on hands and knees at the bottom
of a staircase in the Broadway-Nassau
subway station. He said his head hurt.

He was thirty-seven but looked fifty
as he sat between them on the train,
sober but slurring his words, telling them
every time the car rocked it seemed
he was being kicked in the head.

The next morning his wife took him
to the hospital. Cause of death:
laceration of the brain and a bruise
of the tissues on both sides of the brain.

    *

2016

It's been twenty-eight years
since a neuro-virus found my brain
open to attack. My doctors say

with my history I'm lucky the cognitive
damage is no worse. Lucky to be alive.
When I first saw the scans I thought
my brain looked like cleat-pocked dirt.
At least once a year I dream
I'm standing alone near our end zone
waiting for the kickoff, and the ball
has been tumbling toward me for years
through the air, and I'm aware of my brain
within my skull within my helmet
seeming to throb with knowledge of what
is about to happen as I cradle the ball
at last and begin to run into the fall wind.

At Last

for my brother

We could have finished our ongoing game
of *Careers* abandoned in early 1964
after your tenth trip to the moon.
We could have kept singing the score
of *Kismet* from "Fate" to "Sands of Time"
till we sounded effortless on the harmonies.
We could have remembered the setups
to this scribbled list of punch lines I just found
in a file labeled PHILIP JOKES and we could
have continued our discussion of whether
La Serenata served better clams oreganata
than Mario's before the old chef retired,
whether ham was better eaten hot or cold,
frankfurters with sauerkraut or coleslaw.
We could have settled whether Dean Martin
was better with or without Jerry Lewis
and which Everly Brother was the heart
of the act. I could have gone to Vegas
with you as you wished before you lost
your sight, before you could no longer walk,
before the years of dialysis, and we could
have seen the latest Elvis. I could have learned
to play pai gow poker, your favorite,
and nursed one rye and ginger till our luck
turned. Then we could have shared a room
again after all these years and as we fell asleep
I could have told you of our mother's funeral
nine years after yours, her rages lost at last
in thick clusters and tangles of dementia,
her smile and voice equal parts you and me,
calm as the desert night, an ending I felt
neither of us could possibly have imagined.

Nabokov in Goal, Cambridge, 1919

> I was crazy about goal keeping.
> —Vladimir Nabokov, *Speak, Memory*

He loved to lose himself in the game
opening before him. Breath slowed
as play flowed and he fluttered
in the goal, adjusting socks, knee
guards, gloves, cap. Body checkered
by the net's shadow, he anticipated
angles of attack and grew
calmer as the action approached.

When the ball was downfield
he leaned against a post and closed
his eyes sometimes, knowing
teammates' positions by their calls
and cries. Nabokov spoke so many
tongues that he rejoiced then
in the plain sounds of a kicked ball,
savored the nuance of a foot's impact
on leather. There was also wind
to read, light to keep track of
and the softening autumn grass
turning to mud at midfield.

Nothing that held still was of interest
as he shifted within the goal, aware
but not aware of poems taking shape
in his mind tuned now to no language
ever known. This was the moment
of being lost. He rode its rhythms
long enough to soar across the goal
and catch a shot as it spun and dove
on the arc of its own sizzling flight.

Jules Verne at Safeco Field, Seattle, Spring 2014

On his deathbed Verne vowed to return
in a hundred years. That he is nine years
late he attributes to the way time skews
in the afterlife. That he is in Seattle
instead of Amiens he attributes to the uneven
rush and spin of Earth among the spheres.
The rain he recognizes as a seaport rain,
fine and briny in the early afternoon,
with the screech of gulls borne on gusty
west winds. Foghorns blare in the harbor,
as familiar to him as his own lost breath.
He savors firm ground beneath his feet.

He had foreseen raised roadways curving
over other roadways, skyscrapers with their
structures fully exposed, aircraft that whirl
and hover, that rise straight into the sky.
So too the cacophony of giant machines,
dense smell of fuels, rubble fields clogging
the heart of the city, sleek vessels
skimming above the water's rough surface.

But to see it all at once, to sense its
energy flowing through him, surpasses
his wildest imaginings. He is light
with the pleasure of it, yet he knows
he has come back for more than this,
more than confirmation of his vision
of a changing world. Pounding music mixed
with spoken song cascades around him
from somewhere he cannot determine.
Voices are everywhere, people talking
to the air as they pass through it, gesturing,
colliding, eyes focused wholly inward.
The atmosphere is alive with pulsing colors.

He stands beneath a double-decked
bridge of bright black steel and feels
the current of bodies sweeping past.
He has missed this movement of a crowd.
It carries him inside a vast concrete
arena blazing under strange white lights.
Maybe five hundred lights stacked
almost to the arched roof, far too bright
for his eyes to look at but spellbinding
in their steady otherworldly glow.
Row after row of seats overlook a bowl
of the greenest grass he has ever seen.

He tries to remain in place. The wind
and rain are dwindling as he looks
through walls that are not there,
that are nothing but crossed trusses
and silvering sky open to the elements
though there is a roof afloat above.

Now daylight begins to drift over the field,
its progress slow enough to doubt it is
happening until he turns his gaze upwards.
The roof appears to be folding back into itself
like a telescope. This is something he had
not foreseen! He falls back into a seat
and watches the roof's progress millimeter
by millimeter. He thinks it is like one layer
of heaven pulling back to reveal
a deeper heaven. As it opens, the sun begins
to leave the cover of a cloud and he is
bathed in its slow forgotten warmth.

Childe Hassam at the Oregon Coast, Summer 1904

He woke in the sand and grass of a dune
on Cannon Beach, close to the rocky cove
where he'd worked till dark. Rolling surf
was the sound of pain deep in his head.

Even with his eyes closed he could still
see line after line of foaming breakers
from horizon to shore, cerulean and violet
with hidden life. Everything moved
quickly here at the edge—light, surface
texture, the shapes of land and sea,
structure of cloud. It demanded speed
in return, an art of the moment.

He could not keep up with what he saw.
Flocks of Tufted Puffins soaring south
toward the sea stacks were lost before
he could move his hand. The flicker
of backlit spume against broken clamshells
eluded him. He was too slow for Brown
Pelicans' small shifts against sudden gusts
or the touch and go of Pelagic Cormorants.

But in late afternoon he'd finally felt his limbs
loosen, sensed the day's heat softening
his body from the outside in. When it came,
sleep was a sudden plunge. Dreams swirled
within cyclones of unstable forms and tones.

Now he stood, feeling salt spray soak his scalp,
and turned his back on the incoming tide
to see the sun rise over the Coast Range
as through a scrim of Western Tanager feathers.

At first he thought his cornea must be scored
by wind-blown grit or his vision somehow
tinged by the turbulent moods that returned
with the solstice and drove him out of Boston,

exhausted, unable to think or feel, absorbed
by wayward thoughts. He blinked but the strange
sight remained so he knew this red drenched
in orange, this wild-yellow wash and coal-
black border borrowed from the bird's wings
were exactly what he'd been missing,
what he'd traveled this far west to find.

Yahrzeit

My father died at fifty-three
fifty-three years ago today.

I remember that the morning
after my daughter was born
in the middle of a long September night
my mother responded to the news
by telling me I had been born
in the middle of an even longer night

and on that night my father drove
home from the hospital, lit a cigar
and climbed out the living
room window. He sat on the fire
escape in the company of a dozen
pigeons and finished his fifth
of Cutty Sark and sack of salted filberts.

This was the rare story my mother
told about him that I could
verify because our former neighbor
from the apartment below sent
an email confirming it. For hours
while she and her parents lay awake
my father's feet kept time against
the metal ladder just above them
as he sang "Flat Foot Floogie
(with a Floy Floy)" over and over,
surely in honor of my strange first name.

*

I was named for Flora, my mother's
grandmother. "Flat Foot Floogie
(with a Floy Floy)" was a jazz song

written nine years before I was born,
the year my parents married. The most
common explanation of the title
is that Floy Floy is slang for
a venereal disease and Floogie
really means Floozie. My father
often sang this song while dressing
to go out for dinner with my mother,
his way of making me laugh before
they left. I believe my father
understood what the song was about
but had chosen not to argue
with my mother over yet another
point of contention regarding this child
he never wanted. And whenever he sang
it, I would laugh and my mother
would stalk out of the room.

*

My mother told me
without quite telling me
that my father wanted me
aborted. He knew people, she said.
The mob controlled Red Hook
where he operated his chicken
market, so he knew people.
Italian butchers and bakers
on either side of him. The squeeze,
she said. What did I think,
he got by because he was
a nice guy? Protection money,
the rackets, fix anything,
back room, back alley, back door.
He knew people, my mother told me.

*

I was fourteen when he died
so I have now lived fourteen
years longer than he lived.

Half a year ago, an elderly physician
from New York who as a young man
delivered crates of live poultry to
my father's market in the early 1950s
called to say he was going through
old boxes as he prepared to move
into a retirement community and found
a photograph of my father holding
me in his arms in the courtyard
of our Flatbush apartment building.
He wanted to tell me something
important before he sent the picture:
My father was a lovely man.
And he was so proud of me
because I could recite the entire
Brooklyn Dodgers' lineup, including
uniform numbers and positions,
when I was three years old.

*

I no longer remember the sound
of his voice. I have forgotten how
he laughed. Photos show him
with more hair than I remember,
an actual smile, more weight,
fewer wrinkles on his face, eyeglasses
always held in his hand when posing.
I no longer remember anything

about him that I have not already remembered. Almost all who knew him are gone. If he was still alive he would be one hundred six.

Island

My father was a man of winter night.
He was early darkness, sharp winds, black ice
on the last curve home, and sudden strange light
from a Full Wolf Moon when it starts to rise.
My mother was a woman of force twelve
winds out of nowhere. She was huge waves, air
filled with driving spray, storm feeding on itself
and hurling debris as it hovered there,
a mass of fury, unable to move.
We lived on an island with no bridges
left standing. The mainland was lost in mist
most of the time or glimpsed at the edges
of sight for a second, gaudy as a wish,
out of place, still as nothing else I knew.

Life Bird

Wadsworth Wetlands, Lake County, Illinois

Two old men at the far edge
of the marsh look back at us
through binoculars as we look
at them through binoculars.

Blurred a few yards behind,
a third person turns into
a rolling luggage rack
rigged with camera gear
as I bring him into focus.

We have all come in search
of the same furtive little bird
seen here earlier this morning,
a Least Bittern walking on lily
leaves in the thick August light.
Word went out online and we
have driven fifty miles to add
the Least to my wife's life list.

As the men begin to scan
the shore we hear a harsh
and raspy *wak wak wak*
that means the bird is nearby.
All we can see in the still
water are reeds and bunched
leaves from the place we heard
the call, but the men, crouched
together, have seen something.

We walk the arc of a narrow
path toward them, keeping to
the margins, keeping quiet.

As one man sets up a tripod
the other whispers their welcome
and leads my wife to a spongy
knob of shoreline. He points,
checks his watch, steps back,
and she lifts her binoculars,
breathing deep to steady herself.

The Least Bittern, his pale
buff and white body nestled
in the notch of a lily leaf,
appears like a secret flower
in bloom for just this moment.

She lets her binoculars dangle
and brings her camera up instead.
The bird's golden eye watches her
and I imagine it can sense
her hushed laughter of delight
as an answering call.

Sky Dance

Portland, Oregon

Back from Mexico, the thin
male osprey climbs
through swirling spring wind
to hover over the river.

Banded tail fanned, a fish
dangling from his talons,
he undulates within
the currents. Last year's nest

perched on a power pole
below him is empty still,
but he is sure his mate
must arrive. So he dives

and swoops back up,
crooked wings rippling
as he flies loops within
the fierce echo of his cries.

X.

NEW POEMS

(2016–2024)

Parkinson's

The words I wrote began to shrink
before they reached the line's end
piled in an unreadable scrum.

I told myself it was happening
because I was writing on an uneven
surface, soft surface, cramped surface.
Because the spaces between
my notebook's lines were too narrow
and my pen was too slender.
Because I was tired, needed new
glasses, was rushing to capture
the flow of thought. Because the light
was bad. Because I was in my seventies.

But I already knew it was happening
with any pen on any paper
on any surface in any room
at any time anywhere.

I also knew my voice had begun
to soften, become more breath
than speech, its tone flattened,
pitch unsteady. Swallow, clear
my throat, try again. Must have
a lingering cold, new allergies.
Must be talking too much,
not talking enough. It was
like the way my toes were
beginning to curl, my stride
shrink, my face become a mask.
I was folding into myself, losing
amplitude. On a hike in the woods
my daughter, reaching out for me

when I stumbled, found the word
for me that I could not: Parkinson's.

*

What I knew about
Parkinson's disease was
tremors, slurred speech,
shuffling gait, cramped
posture. I knew about
Michael J. Fox, Linda
Ronstadt, Muhammad Ali,
my cousin Jerry tilted
in a wheelchair with
his face a waxen mask
of the face I remembered.

I did not know
about these surges
of anxiety brought on
by nothing at all
or the way dreams
could come to life
in bed and transform
me into a hissing
panther on all
fours, teeth bared,
one paw lashing
out at my wife.
I never imagined myself
stilled from the inside
out, bloated gut filling
with waste, shoulders blazing
from the least touch of cloth.

*

I can feel my body getting away
from me, becoming erratic and strange.
My fingers and toes are where
I can imagine my brain's garbled signals
land and spark with stray, useless energy.
The months speeding by consist of days
so slow I no longer believe in time.
One of my doctors talks about the endgame,
another the quality of the journey there.
We have no cure for Parkinson's yet,
she tells me, *but we can slow its progression.*
Sometimes, like today, I feel my body
come back to me, trusty scout, bearing
word of exactly what lies ahead.

*

I found myself
one morning near the end
of the year unable to stop
moving, my toes curling
and uncurling, ankles flexing,
fingers rolling over and over
each other, random arm
and leg muscles flickering.
Deep in my body's core,
where there is no
room for it, a tide
of hidden motion surged.
Standing, I swayed
like a man at prayer.
I felt at once chased and

captured, energized
and exhausted, beached
and stuck in a rip current.

    *

The wind is calm this morning as the tide
turns and my wife watches Sanderlings feed
along the shoreline. The rusty mottling
on their backs, thicker bills and shorter wings
tell her these are not Baird's Sandpipers,
but she studies each one just to be sure.

On the softening sand behind her
I am practicing my gait: long strides, strong
arm swings, erect posture, steady pace.
No shuffling! No stumbling! I walk fifty
yards and turn back, looking left and right,
trying not to look down, keeping balance
through my moving body. When we walk
together past the Snowy Plovers' nesting ground,
we see a pair hunkered down side-by-side
in horses' hoof prints facing the oncoming sea.
We stop and I sway a moment before growing still.
For the last half mile I have been straggling
and stumbling as my feet drag through the soft
sand, but my wife's voice adrift in the air draws
me back. As the wind begins to strengthen
I turn to face it and close my eyes, raising one foot
and standing on the unstable beach like the Great
Blue Heron poised ahead of us in the breakers.

    *

The idea was to keep running full stride.
Even as I hit the Long Jump's takeoff board,
even as I moved through the air, I would
keep running. *Don't think,* Coach Gold told me,
but as you sprint, reach for the space
beyond resistance and then be sure
to accelerate more. Never look down
but trust your speed, lean into it
and soar. I remember all of this
now, dream it, as Parkinson's disease
makes the air I move through seem
dense as roiling surf. Snared in a tangle
of dead brain cells, I lumber and lurch,
drawn down into myself, unable to keep
up with my wife when we walk unless
I think about each step, about moving
my arms, lifting my feet, about finding
and following the rhythm of her breath.

*

Two years ago there were still times I could forget
I have Parkinson's disease. I could scramble
up Neahkahnie Mountain, take long hikes
with my wife and daughter, sustain ninety
RPM on my stationary bike for forty minutes.
I did not need to be reminded to stand
straight or swing my arms when I walked.
I could talk and dice carrots at the same time,
turn a screw or open a jar with either hand,
think of that redheaded actor's name,
the one who played Nicholas Brody
on *Homeland*. Some days last year,
thanks to my speech therapist and daily
practice, my voice did not become thin air

in midsentence, or if it did I could rely
on singing "Mack the Knife" to fill
it out again. *Look out,* I could sing,
loud and with notes held beyond
belief, *Look out old Mackie's back.*

*

One drug that was supposed to relax
my rigid muscles froze me in place
instead, unable to lift a fork or swallow a sip
of water. One drug intended to steady
my gait and straighten my posture would
stop working at random, sometimes
as soon as a half hour after I swallowed it,
knocking me down like an inner
linebacker till my wife could haul me up.
Arms around each other, she would drag
me to the couch. One drug made
me slowly tilt to the left until I fell out
of my chair and one drug made me lose
all control of my bowels and one drug
savaged my kidneys and one drug
made my limbs rattle like leaves in wind.
I could not raise my arms high enough
to shampoo my hair. I could not beat
an egg. I could not hold a plate level
when carrying it to the table. I could
not reliably swallow my food. A doctor
phoned to discuss my blood tests
and said *you must be weak as a kitten.*

*

Together my wife, as so often in our life,
brought me back to myself. We spent
two hours walking one mile, stopping when
I had to rest or find my breath. Soon we
could walk the sandy half mile nonstop
to the beach, climb a dune and return
to the car. Then we could walk one mile
on the beach and one mile back
even in the wintry wind. We went
to the basketball court and I began
shooting, at first unable to reach the rim
or even graze the bottom of the net.
She bounce-passed the ball back to me
and cheered. The first time a shot
swished through from the top of the key,
I looked at her and tried to say *that's two*
but the words got lost in her smile.

*

Midstage, almost five years since diagnosis,
five more since the first signs had appeared.
There is no way to forget it anymore.
Better to remember. Along Nehalem Bay,
on a remote marshy trail dense with hidden
roots, we crossed paths with the doctor
who said I must be weak as a kitten, the doctor
who diagnosed my disease, referred me to
my neurologist and had not seen me
in person since then. He looked long
enough to be sure it was me, since I had
lost twenty-five pounds, and all he could
say, looking back the way we had come,
was, *My God, Floyd, how did you get here?*

Early Winter by the Fire

He said the only music he could hear
anymore was the music of stillness.
He told himself it was nothing to fear,
that stillness could be the ultimate dance
he was hearing himself summoned to score.
This was a different kind of melody
than any he had ever known before.
It drifted to a stop. It lurched, changed key,
turned to something like breath where there should be
a cluster of notes. Here, for instance, just
as the passage is about to break free
there is nothing, not even silence. Lost
air, stoppage, notes that have gone so far past
motion they stir only in memory.

Pine Ridge

We live on a ridge of twisted shorepine
and windblown dunegrass. From a mile away
always the pounding of surf and tonight
a fine mist of sand against the windowpane.

This time of year we hear thousands
of Swainson's Thrushes migrate all through
the night. We see fox and elk emerge
from dawnlight, find bird feeders slashed
and tossed aside by a bear whose tracks
lead back into the woods behind our house.

As we walk out into the deepening dark
my wife stops to look up toward the call
of a Saw-whet owl, a sound like steel
against a sharpening stone. She points
east and calls back to him, offering the calm
of soft-whistled toots, face radiant
with the secret light that has been
dazzling me for all our thirty years.

Freestone Peaches

Chip away its crust of time
and his voice sounds the same
as when I last heard him speak
fifty-two years ago. We'd shaken
hands and cuffed shoulders
under the awning of the grocery
where we worked that summer
before college. Our parting words
were promises to keep in touch.

*

Now I have tracked him down,
prompted by seeing my local
grocer's stockboy carry a crate
of freestone peaches. He moved
as though he were my old friend's
shadow, holding the load low
and level as he sidestepped
customers in the produce aisle.
I stood still and recalled laughter
at day's end as we ate peaches
bruised after he'd dropped a crate.

*

He tells me he remembers working
at the grocery but not that I did too.
Only one image remains for him:
forming a chain of six men
to sling watermelons off a truck
and pass them into the store.
Peaches? No, he would not forget
dropping a crate of peaches.

*

What he does remember is working
with me as busboys at a shorefront
restaurant. I remember working
there but not that he did too.
Only one image remains for me:
dropping a tray of soiled dishes
onto the lap of a customer,
the owner firing me in a fury.

*

It is time for him to return
to packing up his home
before next week's move.
Downsizing, retired now,
kids grown and on their own.
Three thousand miles west
it is time for me to prepare
lunch, a few greens, a piece
of last night's roasted chicken,
the freestone peach now ripe
enough to eat. Our parting words
are promises to keep in touch.

Apartment 4M

My childhood room never had enough light,
shadowed by our apartment building's wings,
facing north, curtains drawn, windows shut tight,
hazy with smoke from my brother's Kent Kings.

With the TV and radios always
on, my parents raged in the other two
rooms, filling them with so much noise
I thought for sure that noise must be the true

voice of darkness and silence was a kind
of light. Over time I taught myself to hear
the laughter and jingles hidden behind
my parents' endlessly looping score.

Brooklyn, 1957

Fogged windows, stained drapes,
doors that would no longer close.
Just look, my mother told my father.
Paint flaked and fading, strict lines
of flocked gold and brown wallpaper
starting to wobble. At ten I knew
exactly what was wrong. I was not
fooled by my parents' talk of cheap
landlords, aging finishes, the need
for more space, more light, more air.
I saw its thick cloud roil and seep
into every surface, I saw it where they
never thought to look: late at night
outside our fourth-floor windows
trying to get back in, gathered in lacy
loops above my bedroom closet,
clinging in dark patches to the hallway
lights. I even saw it when we visited
aunts and uncles in their apartments.
I knew we always brought it with us,
let it loose to work the same damage
there. I knew we would bring it with us
when we moved to the rambling house
on a barrier island where I could hear
nearby the steady pounding of surf.

After Terminating Dialysis, June 1997

Our mother came back to him in full
fury the night my brother died.
Blind the last five years, he still saw her
everywhere, flailing his arms as she burst
through the morphine haze, no dose
strong enough to stop her charges.
When he settled a moment, his hair
was a wild white halo on the pillow.
His lips were dry despite the ice chips,
his breath breaking over the rumpled
sheets as light from the solstice moon
streaked his bed. All he ever wanted
was to be as far from her as possible
but here she was in this moonlight
and the darkness it lit, her shrieks filling
the room and the silence beyond them.

Living Night

Because gusting autumn winds
have turned cold and darkness comes
so early, because my cap is pulled low
and the river's rippling surface sounds
like footsteps near the burned-out
dock pilings, I misunderstand what I see
moving through high grass toward me.

At this time of day I expect dogs,
the golden retriever stiff in her hind legs
or Jack Russell frantic at the water's edge.
But this is a shape without firm edges,
a loose and shifting form of living night
my mind turns into a shadowy being,
equally man and evening mist.

The figure huddled into itself now bears
a tousled beard and glares at me
with eyes I had not been able to see.
Though he makes no sound the air
above me whispers in a language
I do not know. But I do know who this is.

Nights like these, Dickens walked
beside any river he could find, burning
off energy, savoring the lack of clarity
around him, acrid breath, the absence
of speech. In a world gone murky
he could cloak himself in memory,
or step free of all that familial light
and become the story of his own
inner life. Hidden current called him,
and the slow spin of driftwood,
the distant thrum of an unseen vessel's
engine working its way upstream,

a raptor's cry. Exhaustion called him,
and darkness he swallowed whole.

I reach the place where crumbled rock
and rubble are dumped to cap the toxic
riverbank. The gouged land runs
sheer to the water, and I have come
far enough north for downtown light
to seep through the dark and let me
know I am alone again. Just offshore,
a barge squats under its load of heavy
equipment, ready for morning.

NOTES

Approaching Winter

"October 30, 1938": On Halloween night—October 30, 1938—*The Mercury Theatre on the Air* broadcast Orson Welles's radio production of *The War of the Worlds*, a story of alien invasion originally published by H. G. Wells in 1898. Presented as though it were live, breaking news, *The War of the Worlds* fooled listeners into believing giant Martian creatures had landed in New Jersey and were slaughtering their way toward New York. According to the next day's *New York Times*, "a wave of mass hysteria seized thousands of radio listeners" and "disrupted households, interrupted religious services, created traffic jams and clogged communications systems."

"Crying over 'Scarlet Ribbons'": The popular song "Scarlet Ribbons (For Her Hair)" was written in 1949 by Evelyn Danzig and Jack Segal. It tells the story of a father desperate but unable—until a final miracle—to find the hair ribbons his daughter prays for. When I was young, I listened to the version sung by Harry Belafonte so many times that it became one of those brainworm tunes hooked in my memory.

"Dylan Thomas at Sundown, November 9, 1953": Dylan Thomas died on November 9, 1953, at the age of thirty-nine.

"Samuel Beckett Throws Out the First Pitch": Samuel Beckett was an excellent cricket player as a young man. He appeared in two games for Dublin University, the only Nobel Prize–winning author to have played first-class cricket or to be featured in the *Wisden Cricketers' Almanack*. In August 1957, the Brooklyn Dodgers were owned by Walter O'Malley and were in their final weeks of existence before leaving the borough to become the Los Angeles Dodgers. Roy Campanella was their Hall of Fame catcher. Though they should have happened, the events in this poem are imaginary.

Far West

"Chris Cagle Is Dead": Christian "Red" Cagle (1905–1942) played four years of college football at the Southwestern Louisiana Institute, then four more years at the U.S. Military Academy, where he was team captain and a three-time All-American halfback. Cagle was such an electrifying, versatile, and dominant runner-passer that he was featured on the cover of *Time* during his senior year at Army. He turned pro in 1930 and played five seasons for the New York Giants and Brooklyn Dodgers football teams. Notorious for playing without a helmet or wearing one with its chin strap loose, Cagle must have absorbed countless concussion-producing hits during his thirteen-year career. Such repeated head trauma, and the peculiar circumstances of his death at thirty-seven, when he was found at the bottom of a New York subway staircase complaining of head pain, suggest that—while he may have slipped on ice or fallen down the stairs after drinking too much on the day after Christmas—he might actually have been suffering from chronic traumatic encephalopathy (CTE), the degenerative brain disease now recognized as being associated with football-related head injury.

"Jules Verne at Safeco Field, Seattle, Spring 2014": As far as I know, the extraordinary French novelist did not make a vow to return from the afterlife a hundred years after his death in 1905. But I believe he would have loved to have a look at our world, especially the kinds of mechanical wonders—such as Safeco Field's retractable roof—that he was inspired to imagine.

"Childe Hassam at the Oregon Coast, Summer 1904": The American Impressionist painter Frederick Childe Hassam (1859–1935), a New England native, first came to Oregon in 1904 after a period of depression and serious drinking. He spent time painting landscapes in the Cascade Mountains, the deserts east of the mountains, the city of Portland, and the north Oregon coast in and around Cannon Beach.

FLOYD SKLOOT's recent collections of poetry, *The End of Dreams* (2006), *The Snow's Music* (2008), *Approaching Winter* (2015), and *Far West* (2019), were published by Louisiana State University Press. *The End of Dreams* was a finalist for the Paterson Prize, and *Far West* received LSU Press's L. E. Phillabaum Poetry Award. In 2010, *Poets & Writers* named him one of fifty of the most inspiring writers in the world. Also a memoirist and fiction writer, Skloot boasts numerous awards, including three Pushcart Prizes, the PEN USA Literary Award, and two Pacific Northwest Booksellers Book Awards. He lives with his wife, Beverly Hallberg, in Portland and in Manzanita, Oregon, and is the father of Rebecca Skloot, author of the internationally acclaimed 2010 bestseller *The Immortal Life of Henrietta Lacks*.